How to Profit
from the
Coming Rapture

How to Profit from the Coming Rapture

Getting Ahead When You're Left Behind

Steve and Evie Levy as told to
Ellis Weiner and Barbara Davilman

Illustrations by Mark Adam Abramowicz

Little, Brown and Company
New York Boston London

Disclaimer: We absolutely guarantee that the investment and financial advice in this book will bring you wealth, security, and success—*but only once the Rapture takes place and is followed by the Tribulation.* (And provided that you're still alive and on Earth.) Until then, just hang on. Study our recommendations, take notes, make a plan. But don't actually do anything that we suggest until the faithful are swept up to meet Jesus in the sky and the seven-year run-up to the end of civilization—or, rather, *this* civilization—gets under way.

Steve and Evie Levy

Disclaimer of the Disclaimer: The preceding Disclaimer is fraudulent, nonbinding, invalid, and completely bogus. Its "guarantee" of wealth, security, and success, whether during the Rapture and the Tribulation or at any other time, should be ignored. This book is for entertainment purposes only and should not be construed as offering any actual financial advice whatsoever. Steve and Evie Levy have no financial expertise. In terms of investments and the accumulation of personal wealth, they don't know what they're talking about. In fact, they don't even exist. We should know. We made them up.

Ellis Weiner and Barbara Davilman

Little, Brown and Company
Hachette Book Group
237 Park Avenue, New York, NY 10017
Visit our Web site at www.HachetteBookGroup.com

First Edition: November 2008

Little, Brown and Company is a division of Hachette Book Group, Inc. The Little, Brown name and logo are trademarks of Hachette Book Group, Inc.

Library of Congress Cataloging-in-Publication Data
Weiner, Ellis.
　　How to profit from the coming Rapture: getting ahead when you're left behind / Steve and Evie Levy, as told to Ellis Weiner and Barbara Davilman.
　　　　p. cm.
　　Includes bibliographical references.
　　ISBN-13: 978-0-316-01730-5
　　ISBN-10: 0-316-01730-2
　　1. Rapture (Christian eschatology)—Humor.　2. Finance, Personal—Humor.
I. Davilman, Barbara.　II. Title.
　　PN6231.R353W45 2008
　　818'.5407—dc22　　2008009553

10 9 8 7 6 5 4 3 2 1

RRD-IN

Printed in the United States of America

Contents

Foreword vii

How to Read This Book ix

Rapture-Tribulation Time Line xii

PART I: Run-up to Rapture 1

PART II: The Rapture 15

PART III: The Tribulation: The Seal Judgments 27

PART IV: The Tribulation: The Trumpet Judgments 99

PART V: The Tribulation: The Bowl Judgments 139

PART VI: One Wedding and an Apocalypse 167

PART VII: Two Happy Endings 183

Our Sources 207

Acknowledgments 209

Foreword

The Rapture is coming.

The Tribulation, a horrifying nightmare of bloodshed and destruction, will follow.

And that means one thing: investment opportunities!

When you hear "End Times," think "Good Times." It's as though these two events—the sudden flying-up to Heaven of all Fundamentalist Dispensationalist Premillennialist Evangelical Christians, and the seven-year period of travail and disaster that climaxes in the Battle of Armageddon and the Second Coming of Jesus Christ—were specifically created not only to reward a specific Christian sect with an early ticket to Paradise, but to provide the rest of us (i.e., everybody else on Earth) with a big truckload of moneymaking possibilities, if we survive. And we can't wait to share them with you.

In the pages that follow, we'll walk you through the many dramatic events and spectacular disasters that God has in store for those of us "left behind," from the early appearances of false messiahs to the final triumph, when Christ rules on Earth for a thousand years and Satan is cast into the Lake of Fire. And we'll show you how to exploit those events to attain a wide range of financial goals.

You'll learn how to earn extra cash—and exactly what kinds of supplies and weapons to spend it on. We'll teach you how to start your own business and make it work—even as your customer base (anyone who wasn't Raptured away) is dying off by the millions. We'll give you the facts and the strategies to weather the ups and downs of the markets and the rise and fall and re-rise and re-fall of the Antichrist.

When people ask us if we "believe in" the Rapture, we answer: How can you not, when tens of millions of our countrymen are sure it's coming, and a 2004 *Newsweek* poll found that *55 percent* of Americans believed that "before the world ends, the religiously faithful will be saved and taken to Heaven"?

So, yes, we think the Rapture could take place at any moment. But are we prepared for it? Having accepted these facts, have we also accepted Christ as our personal savior, so as to be "saved" and ready to go when the skies open and He appears?

Our answer may disappoint some, but here it is:

We haven't. We can't. We're Jews.

Don't get us wrong. We believe that Jesus was a nice young man who said a lot of important things. But we just don't believe He was the Messiah, and so we simply cannot convince ourselves to worship Him in the way we're told we should.

Of course, this means that when the Rapture happens we'll remain here on Earth, in our bodies, as we normally are. But we won't be alone. Billions of others (and not just Jews) all around the world will be left behind, too (at least for a while), to witness and take part in (and, sadly, in some cases, get horribly killed by) one of the most exciting and fascinating eras in human history. It will be a time of turmoil, and a time of bloodshed, and a time of natural catastrophe such as the world has never seen. But it will also be a time filled with potential, exploding with unique opportunities for the smart investor and the bold entrepreneur.

That is why we have written this book.

Steve and Evie Levy
Beverly Hills, CA

How to Read This Book

We have organized *How to Profit from the Coming Rapture* chronologically, from the earliest signs proving that the End Times are here, or almost here, through the Seal, Trumpet, and Bowl Judgments, to the Second Coming and the Millennium, and concluding with the New Heaven and the New Earth—and we want to help you profit from every minute of it.

For this reason, and because our financial advice will be predicated on events that will, without question, happen in the future, *we urge you to read this book in order, front to back, and not "jump around."* In this way, not only will you be introduced to our investment and entrepreneurial tips in the proper sequence, but you'll also experience the mounting drama of a chapter-by-chapter synopsis of the events of the Rapture and the Tribulation.

Each chapter will include these sections:

+ A Description of What Will Happen and When, according to the Bible
+ Supporting Biblical Documentation, which will be cited and, in some cases, quoted
+ An Explanation of the Event, to place it in the context of what has come before and to elaborate on its details

✦ Our Financial Advice for that particular event or time period, under the heading **"FOR NOW."** We often follow these with recommendations on how to take advantage of *future* developments (the certainty of which is never in doubt) under the heading **"FOR LATER."** In both categories we'll suggest entrepreneurial ventures you can start yourself, under the heading **"MIND YOUR OWN BUSINESS."**

Bear in mind that when we describe developments that "will occur in the future," we mean literally that. We won't be referring to things that "could" happen. We won't be talking about "trends" or "possible outcomes." These things are going to happen, period.

How can we be so sure? Because the Bible says so. Thanks to the Good Book, *we know the precise events that are going to take place from now until "the end of the world."*

What we won't know are the exact casualty statistics.

It is part of our Heavenly Father's marvelous plan that billions of us be brutally slaughtered. The "body count" will be steadily changing, and it may be hard to remember at any given moment how many people are left alive—if any! But the Bible is frustratingly inexact in its tally of the living and the dead, and it doesn't take into account the number of people who will be born during the seven years under discussion.

Still, we will occasionally try to give a rough estimate of the changes in the world's population. We start by calculating how many people will experience the Rapture and be removed from the Earth prior to the Tribulation. (We address the contentious issue of whether or not the Rapture really *will* be "prior" to the Tribulation later in the text.)

We begin with the widely agreed-on estimate that the Earth's population as of the end of 2007 was around 6.6 billion. From this Web site: http://www.gcts.edu/ockenga/globalchristianity/

resources.php . . . we get the total number of Christians (or, at least, "church members") worldwide as of mid-2007: 2,077,909,000.

From a survey conducted in ten countries (in North America, Latin America, Africa, and Asia) by the Pew Forum in 2006 on world Pentecostalism here: http://pewforum.org/publications/surveys/pentecostals-06.pdf . . . we get the percentage of "Christians" who answered "yes" to the question "Do you believe in the Rapture?" The average of those ten figures is 70 percent, from which we're entitled to estimate that 70 percent of world Christians believe in the Rapture. (Sixty-three percent of all American Christians do.)

We assume, since it's none of our business to judge people's sincerity of faith, that those who believe in the Rapture will, in fact, be Raptured. Thus, the number of people who will fly to join Jesus in the sky when the Rapture occurs is 2,077,909,000 × 70% = 1,454,536,300 . . . or around 22 percent of the world population.

That leaves a whopping 5,145,463,700 people still on Earth to experience the Tribulation. Odds are that you and your family will be among them. Keep reading, and you'll be perfectly prepared to take advantage of these events, to assure the financial security of yourself and your loved ones from the moment the Rapture occurs to that glorious time, one thousand and seven years later, when God leaves Heaven and moves down to live with man on Earth.

Rapture-Tribulation Time Line

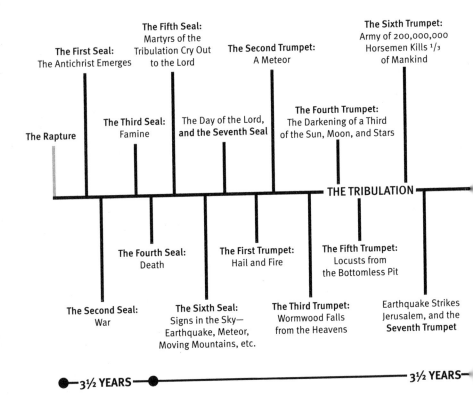

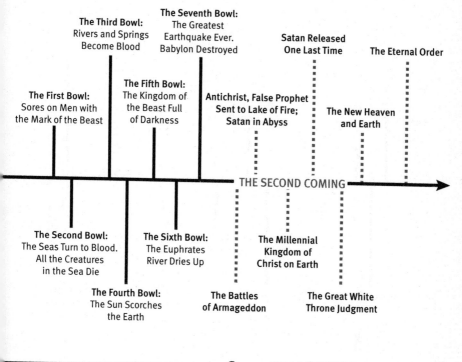

The Third Bowl:
Rivers and Springs
Become Blood

The Seventh Bowl:
The Greatest
Earthquake Ever.
Babylon Destroyed

Satan Released
One Last Time

The Eternal Order

The First Bowl:
Sores on Men with
the Mark of the Beast

The Fifth Bowl:
The Kingdom of
the Beast Full
of Darkness

Antichrist, False Prophet
Sent to Lake of Fire;
Satan in Abyss

The New Heaven
and Earth

THE SECOND COMING

The Second Bowl:
The Seas Turn to Blood.
All the Creatures
in the Sea Die

The Sixth Bowl:
The Euphrates
River Dries Up

The Millennial
Kingdom of
Christ on Earth

The Fourth Bowl:
The Sun Scorches
the Earth

The Battles
of Armageddon

The Great White
Throne Judgment

● 1,000 YEARS ● ETERNITY

Part I **Run-up to Rapture**

CHAPTER 1

Israel Reestablished

(And a Few Notes on Financial Terms)

The Rapture can occur at any time. The subsequent Tribulation, however, cannot begin until the Antichrist (i.e., Satan's representative on Earth, about whom more later) signs a pact with Israel. Thus, in order for there to be a Tribulation — and the Apocalypse, the Second Coming, and the Millennium — there has to be a State of Israel. No wonder Christians the world over rejoiced in 1948.

> The Tribulation officially begins when the Antichrist, as head of a world government, makes a seven-year covenant with Israel. That is why the creation of the State of Israel in 1948 was so wonderful for Christians as well as Jews. It set the stage for everything to come and fulfilled various prophecies, including Zephaniah 2:1–2, Ezekiel 38–39, and Isaiah 11:11–12.

Once Israel came into existence, Fundamentalist Dispensationalist Premillennialist Evangelical Christians the world over brought new vigor to a tireless vigil that continues to this very day, waiting and hoping for the end of the world. Who wouldn't, when you expect it to bring eternal salvation?

We're kind of looking forward to it, too, because we've got lots of financial plans ready to go once the seven-year Tribulation clock starts ticking. But before we can put them into action, we (and you) will have to rethink certain basic financial concepts. Here are the most important:

1. Time Frame: Normally, in financial matters, "long-term" refers to periods of time measurable in decades, and "short-term" investments usually last between one and five years. Seven years after the Tribulation begins, however, all investments will be over and most of the human race will be dead. *And no one except readers of this book will know this is happening.* (The Fundamentalist Christians who would know it will be in Heaven by then.) Therefore, by drastically compressing your time sense, you can obtain a significant advantage over the market.

   That's why, once the Rapture happens, we want you to fine-tune your vocabulary so that

   ✔ "long-term" refers to anything lasting more than one year;
   ✔ "medium-term" refers to anything lasting between two and twelve months;
   ✔ "the near future" refers to anything taking place from the day after tomorrow until about two months later;
   ✔ "short-term" refers to anything starting now-ish and lasting until the end of the day, or maybe into the next morning on the West Coast;
   ✔ "immediately" refers to anything that as soon as you say "immediately" is twenty minutes too late, so never mind.

   Result? While everyone else continues the habit of talking about "realizing steady growth over the ensuing ten-year cycle," you'll be talking about "getting a bunch of money on Thursday." And making it happen!

2. "Rainy-Day" Liquid Reserve: Today, many financial advisers suggest keeping enough money to cover about eight months' worth of expenses in a readily available form, usually a money market fund. This is commonly called a "rainy-day reserve," which is probably why such cash is referred to as being "liquid."

However, during the Tribulation, cash will be worth less and less, and *liquids themselves* will become more valuable. So use your reserve of liquid cash now to prepare your cache of reserved liquids (bottled water, soft drinks, alcoholic beverages, fruit juice, et cetera) for later.

3. Life Insurance: Most people don't need life insurance until they either get married or have children, and by then they can't afford to die. Bear in mind that once the Rapture takes place, the odds of anyone dying at any given time will be far less than the odds of almost everyone dying at once. Therefore, we recommend that you buy all the coverage you can afford. On everyone you know.

Shop around. Compare whole life for a limited term versus term for a whole lifetime. That way, if you survive, you'll be at least a little more glad to be alive.

4. Wills: Normally, a will is something carefully compiled in a spirit of solemnity and serious thought and only changed sporadically, over decades. This, of course, is because the prospect of our death feels both unpleasant to think about and remote in terms of its likelihood.

During the Tribulation, however, death—of your loved ones, your heirs and assigns, and even yourself—will be a daily part of life. Therefore, once the Rapture takes place, learn to think of your will not as a monumental document to be revised sporadically, if at all, but as a kind of ongoing, post-humous "to do" list. Post it on the refrigerator with attractive or whimsical magnets. Maybe clip a colorful, fun felt-tip pen to it for added convenience. Revisit it every day or even every few hours; modify and revise and "touch it up" to keep pace with your changing moods and circumstances. Consider employing a notary public in your home.

If you take the advice in the pages that follow, your estate will increase even as your list of people to leave it to is shrinking. Get into the habit of updating your will today and eventually you, or whoever you love and is left alive after you, will be glad you did.

CHAPTER 2

Signs of the (End) Times

We know the Last Days are coming, if not actually here, because events around the world today have been predicted by various books of the Bible in remarkable detail.

The following chart lists some prescient predictions from Scripture, the relevant chapters and verses, and examples drawn from contemporary life. The accuracy of these prophecies speaks for itself.

BIBLICAL PROOF THAT THE END IS NEAR

Predicted Phenomenon	Scriptural Citation	Characterized by . . .	Contemporary Examples
Godlessness	2 Timothy 3:1–7	Men shall be lovers of their own selves, covetous, boasters, proud, blasphemers, disobedient to parents, unthankful, unholy	Just about everybody we know, plus our kids
False messiahs and false prophets	Matthew 24:5, 24:11	Deceiving many	David Koresh, Jim Jones, Sun Myung Moon, Bhagwan Shree Rajneesh, L. Ron Hubbard, Pat Robertson, Warren Jeffs, Jerry Falwell, George W. Bush

CONTINUED ON NEXT PAGE

CONTINUED FROM PREVIOUS PAGE

Predicted Phenomenon	Scriptural Citation	Characterized by ...	Contemporary Examples
Wars and rumors of wars	Matthew 24:6	Will come to pass, but the end is not yet (i.e., there will be wars, but not *the* War)	The War on Poverty, the Cola Wars, the War on Drugs, the War on Terror, the Culture War, the War on Christmas, the War on Illegal Immigration
Famines, pestilences, earthquakes	Matthew 24:7	In divers places	Famine in Africa; food riots in Haiti, Bangladesh, Egypt; bee colony collapse around the US; earthquakes in Indonesia, Central America, California, and China; cyclone in Myanmar; also Hurricane Katrina, rats in Manhattan, and little earthquakes we can't remember

 **FOR NOW**

Obviously, if the Last Days haven't started by now, they probably will tomorrow. So we want you to invest accordingly.

IN GODLESSNESS WE TRUST

Buy stock in companies that service the godlessness sector. Look for

* companies that provide goods and services that godly people disapprove of, or at least say they disapprove of, such as liquor, pornography, gambling (horse racing, "gaming," lotteries), and condoms and other forms of birth control;
* anything involved with "our godless secular culture," such as television, movies, popular music, video games, graphic novels, Broadway, Off Broadway, Off Off Broadway, regional

theater, dance, puppet shows, cartoons, stand-up comedy, and clip art on placemats in diners;

* companies that serve or help to advance the gay agenda;
* anything scientific;
* companies that publish books by, about, or for atheists, feminists, liberals, wizards, intellectuals, urban sophisticates, vampires, serial killers, Europeans, Gen X, Gen Y, Gen Z, and any other Gen that comes along.

PROFIT FROM PROPHETEERING™

The craze for ordinary people to present themselves as either a prophet of God or as the Messiah Himself offers excellent opportunities for the small entrepreneur. Here are two businesses you can start with a minimal outlay of capital, as part of an approach we call Propheteering:

1. **TGID ("Thank God It's Doomsday"):** As you'll see in later chapters, when the Antichrist arises, he will be assisted by someone the Bible refers to as the False Prophet. Until then, however, a series of bogus messengers of God will emerge whom the Bible also refers to as "false prophets." For the sake of clarity we will refer to these fraudulent prophets as "phony prophets." Here is a clever, legal, and low-cost way to realize authentic profits from phony prophets:

☞ Find a phony prophet and his followers (Google "Christian prophet" and skim the 1,790,000 Web sites). Wait until he or she predicts a specific day on which the world will end.

☞ Two weeks before the appointed date, move into the phony prophet's neighborhood and rent several self-storage units and a panel truck or a van. Hire two strong college kids.

☞ Advertising it as a "Doomsday Buy-a-Thon," visit the "prophet's" followers and offer to buy their appliances, home electronics, et cetera, for cash. Offer lowball prices and bottom dollar. (Sample sales line: "What do you need a washer-dryer for? You're going to Heaven!") Store their items in your rented lockers, taking special care to note who owned what.

☞ Wait for the predicted end of the world to come and go without incident—which, of course, it will. Remember, this is a phony prophet, not a real one.

☞ Return to the faithful with a big "Red-Letter Redemption Event." Let them "redeem" their former possessions at a nice markup. If, for example, you bought Jim and Donna's thirty-eight-inch Panasonic TV for $100, sell it back to them for $175. Be sure to remind them that they're not buying "a pig in a poke." They're purchasing *their own stuff.*

☞ Pay the college kids, pocket your profits, and get out of town.

☞ Repeat elsewhere.

2. Savior Self: When it comes to false messiahs, there will be two kinds of people: those who truly think they are the Messiah, and those who know they're not but want others to think they are. Either way, they're going to need props, costumes, and other supplies—which you can provide.

💲 MIND YOUR OWN BUSINESS

- You call it: Messiah-in-a-Box or "Mess" Kits
- You sell: Complete outfits for self-proclaimed messiahs
- You offer: Gear and props for all aspects of the role, including:

The Walk: The most successful messiahs wear some sort of Middle Eastern robe and crude sandals *but not flip-flops.* Your customers will also appreciate the "Desert Madman" glue-on beard and "Wandering the Wilderness" shepherd's staff

---

or crook. But people have also become familiar with other messianic "looks" as well, including the Messiah from Outer Space (jumpsuit, Nikes).

The Talk: No one will give the time of day — let alone lifelong religious devotion — to a "messiah" who talks like Ryan Seacrest or Miss South Carolina. Include a list of Useful Messianic Phrases that can be employed not only in preaching but in everyday conversation, such as "Rejoice, and be exceedingly glad, for behold: Flank steak is on sale," and "Suffer the little children to come unto me, that I may give unto them a time out, that they might shut up for five lousy minutes."

The Gawk: Include a chart (or, better, an instructional DVD) of Basic Holy Facial Expressions, including "Woe at Man's Sinfulness," "Righteous Wrath at the Unholy," "Infinite Pity for the Oppressed," "High Indignation at Hypocrites," and "Staring Off into Space, Overwhelmed by Love for Mankind."

WAR? HOT DOG!

As everyone knows, you can't go wrong investing in companies that profit from war (weapons and tech companies, uniform manufacturers, et cetera). But you now know there will be *rumors of war*. By investing accordingly, you can get a real jump on the market.

Start with the obvious — survival goods, such as duct tape, home medical kits, bottled water, self-powered radios, and electric generators. Where do people buy these items? Increasingly, they do so at national chains like Home Depot and Lowe's. So a "basic rumors-of-war" investment is in hardware retailers.

Then take it a step further. If national hardware chains are going to thrive as war rumors spread, who else will? That's right:

all the little snack wagons that appear in front of those big mega–hardware stores to service the customer traffic. Here, then, is an investment tip right from the Bible: The more rumors of war there are, the more people will buy hot dogs—which means the more you should invest in snack cart supplies.

The graph below offers our suggestion as to how to apportion your rumors-of-war snack cart portfolio.

INVESTING IN RUMORS OF WAR: SAMPLE SNACK CART PORTFOLIO

■ Hot Dogs	■ Buns
□ Mustard (Yellow)	■ Mustard (Spicy)
■ Relish	■ Sauerkraut
■ Hamburgers	■ Ketchup

As you can see, we decided to put the balance of our hypothetical stake in "Hot Dogs," which are a perennial favorite with kids as well as adults, and "Buns," which includes both hot dog and hamburger buns. You may disagree. You may, for example, wish to eliminate "Sauerkraut" entirely and focus more on the "Hamburgers" component of the snack cart sector if you somehow happen to know that your community prefers ground beef. Feel free to adjust the numbers to suit your personal investment style.

FOR LATER ⏱

PRE-NEED ARRANGEMENTS

We keep saying, "The Rapture is coming," so you're entitled to ask, "Great—so how can I make money on that knowledge *now*, before it actually takes place?"

Good question. And we have an answer.

The people who expect themselves to be Raptured up constitute a highly specific customer base. In all this excitement, they might not (understandably) have thought of one thing: Who is going to tidy up their affairs *once they're gone?*

Meaning: Who will take care of their un-Raptured pets, feeding and loving them for the rest of their lives, or placing them in loving, if less devoutly Christian, homes? Their friends? Their relatives? But they'll be Raptured, too. Either that or they'll be too devastated to do much more than cry out to the Lord with great lamentation.

That's where you can provide a valuable service.

🐷$ MIND YOUR OWN BUSINESS

- You call it: PerPETual Care
- You sell: Post-Rapture pet care policies, renewable annually
- You offer: Care and feeding of the pet for its lifetime *or* guaranteed placement in a loving, safe home

Start local, expand to regional, then maybe franchise it nationally.

FEARFULLY ASKED QUESTIONS (FAQ)

Q. I'm about to buy a home. Should I opt for an adjustable-rate mortgage (ARM), on the assumption that it will only go up a little, because Jesus will come within seven years and pay it off for me?

A. No. Although the Rapture is imminent, we don't know exactly when it will take place, and you could be facing several rate increases on your ARM before it gets here.

Besides, even when the Tribulation ends and Jesus does arrive, He will *not* pay off your mortgage. We may not be Christians, but even we know that that's not what He is "all about." Therefore we suggest getting a fixed-rate mortgage with a monthly payment you know you will be able to afford until the end of the world. But if you haven't yet gotten into the real estate market, stay out. Why sink your cash into a down payment and the upkeep of a house if apocalyptic devastation is around the corner? Keep renting.

Q. I'm interested in investing in godlessness. Where can I get a copy of the Gay Agenda?

A. In any religious bookstore.

Part II The Rapture

CHAPTER 3

Up, Up, and Away

Some people question the very reality of the Rapture because, they point out, the word *rapture* doesn't appear in any English translation of the Bible. And that's true. It doesn't.

But as writers of many books, we know how easy it is for words to get lost or misplaced when you're going from one draft to the next, and from one language to another. Considering how old the Bible is, and how many drafts it probably went through, it's amazing more words didn't get left out. Besides, the words *e-mail, playoffs,* and *Botox* don't appear in the Bible, either, and we know they refer to real things.

By the way, there will be many who question our discussion of the Rapture *here,* at this point in the chronology. There is widespread disagreement over when the Rapture will occur with regard to the seven-year-long Tribulation. One opinion (the so-called Mid-Trib view) holds that the Rapture will not take place until halfway through the Tribulation. Those who subscribe to the Pre-Wrath view believe that the Rapture will occur three-quarters of the way into the Tribulation, and the Post-Trib school insists that the Rapture will occur only at the very end of the Tribulation. There are other, more esoteric views as well.

We're sticking with the Pre-Trib notion that the Rapture will precede and herald the Tribulation. It seems to be the most widely accepted and is the one illustrated in the Left Behind books.

(These novels, written by pastor Tim LaHaye and writer Jerry B. Jenkins, began in 1995 with *Left Behind*, about a band of plucky Christians who find themselves still on Earth after the Rapture has transported some of their loved ones to Heaven. Over the course of twelve sequels, airline pilot Rayford Steele and other characters struggle to survive as the Tribulation unfolds. The series also includes three prequels, several graphic novels, and, for younger readers, twelve Left Behind for Kids titles. In all, the franchise has sold more than 65 million books. We can't argue with those kinds of numbers. If the Rapture is Pre-Trib to the Left Behind community, it's Pre-Trib to us, too.)

Having said all that, we face the basic question: *What makes anyone think there will be a Rapture at all?*

The description of the Rapture comes mainly in three quotes from Scripture: 1 Corinthians 15:51–54 (*52: In a moment, in the twinkling of an eye, at the last trump: for the trumpet shall sound, and the dead shall be raised incorruptible, and we shall be changed*), 1 Thessalonians 4:16–17 (*16: For the Lord himself shall descend from heaven with a shout, with the voice of the archangel, and with the trump of God: and the dead in Christ shall rise first. 17: Then we which are alive and remain shall be caught up together with them in the clouds, to meet the Lord in the air: and so shall we ever be with the Lord*), and John 14:2–3.

Who Gets to Go

Only Christians will be eligible to be Raptured to Heaven, but not just any Christians. This experience will be reserved for those who have been "saved"—i.e., who have admitted that they are sinners, have conceded that they can be redeemed only by allowing Christ into their hearts, have embraced the idea that salvation is a matter of faith alone (and not "works"), and have accepted Christ as their personal savior. Catholics, in other words—with their huge church hierarchy, their pope, their confession and absolution and so forth—are not included. Most Protestants are not included, either.

In fact, pretty much no one is included except Fundamentalist Dispensationalist "born again" Protestants. Of course, anyone, of any religion, plus atheists, can join this group whenever they wish, simply by "coming to Jesus."

What Will Happen

In the Pre-Tribulation view, the Rapture is "imminent." That means it can occur at any time, without special warnings or mystical signs. This is why people who believe in the Rapture are so happy and loving and righteous *all the time*. They know that at any second they can be lifted up off the Earth and transported to Heaven!

When they are, here, to the best of our understanding, is how it will happen.

First, the people who accepted Jesus as their savior (throughout all of history) but who are currently dead will rise up from their graves, shedding anything not natural that is still on or in their bodies, or at least whatever is left of their bodies. This includes everything from toupees to pacemakers, from jewelry to tattoos, from the fillings in their teeth to the polish on their nails to the steel plates in their heads.

The remains of the dead will fly up into the sky, where Jesus will greet them. Then the same thing will happen to the living who have been "saved." They will be naked, although at some point both the physical bodies of the living and the remains of the dead will be replaced with "soul bodies." Jesus will escort these believers (collectively known as "the Church") to Heaven, where they will reside until the end of the seven-year Tribulation.

Note that in 1 Corinthians 15:52, this trip to Heaven is described as lasting "a moment," and will occur "in the twinkling of an eye." For that reason, traditional depictions of this event start with the Rapture as a fait accompli. It is invisible and instantaneous. No one sees it happen. The faithful simply disappear, in an instant, leaving behind only their earthly belongings.

But we are now proud to present a new Rapture timetable.

The Six-Minute Rapture

It is possible, using strictly biblical sources, to interpret the interval of "a moment" and "the twinkling of an eye" as lasting more—*much more*—than an instant. This discovery, which we have made and which is explained here for the first time anywhere, is not only important to those who wish to profit from the coming Rapture, but will quite possibly be reassuring to anyone worried about being "left behind" and unable to offer a final farewell to his or her loved ones who are swept up to Heaven.

Here is what we have discovered:

One of the most important scriptural verses concerning the Tribulation comes from the book of Daniel, chapter 9, starting with verse 24 (*Seventy weeks are determined upon thy people and upon thy holy city, to finish the transgression, and to make an end of sins, and to make reconciliation for iniquity, and to bring in everlasting righteousness, and to seal up the vision and prophecy, and to anoint the most Holy*). This "seventy-week" period begins with the restoration of Jerusalem.

Most scholars and theologians believe that these "weeks" are to be thought of not in terms of days but in terms of years—each "week" lasts seven years. Well, it occurred to us that if the Bible uses "day" to mean "year" and "week" to mean "a period of seven years," maybe it also uses other chronological terms in nonliteral ways that can be interpreted.

The much-longed-for, long-awaited salvation of the Six-Minute Rapture
(Not shown: Jesus, in clouds, welcoming remains of the dead)

And so we started thinking: When one day means one year, what you do is multiply one day by 360. (While in reality a year equals 365.25 days, many people believe that in prophecy a year is taken to mean 360 days.) We think you can apply a similar calculation to the duration of the Rapture. Assuming "the twinkling of an eye" to be roughly equal to one second, then an application of biblical arithmetic suggests that the Rapture will actually last 360 seconds, or *six minutes!*

Rather than simply vanish, the Rapturees will drift—or zoom—upward, naked, in full view of the world. Of course, we don't know how fast they will rise, because their destination will be to join Jesus, whose altitude is unspecified in Scripture. The higher He is, the faster they'll have to go. If, for example, Jesus hovers above the Earth at the height of normal commercial airline flight (say, 32,000 feet, which is about six miles), then in order to meet Him in six minutes, the Rapturees will have to soar skyward at a velocity of approximately sixty miles per hour.

But what if, as we expect, He hovers at a more convenient altitude? Say, a thousand feet? Then the Raptured ones will rise at a leisurely, dreamy 1.89 miles per hour. Those left below will have at least some time in which to make their farewells, to realize who has been selected and who has not, to ask important last-minute questions such as "Where did you leave the checkbook?" and "Can I have your iPod?" and to wish the lucky Rapturees "Bon voyage" and so forth. And that's a comfort.

Whether the Rapture lasts six minutes or a single instant, its effects will continue for days. During that time, while the world is reeling and everyone is struggling to figure out what has happened and what will happen next, you (our reader) will be prepared. Here are a few suggestions for making some short-term and longer-term profits.

⏱ FOR NOW

CELEBRATE THE MOMENTS OF THEIR LIFT

Get into the habit of carrying with you, at all times, a decent still camera, or at least a cell phone that takes photos. You'll be positioned to make a quick financial killing once the Rapture begins.

🐷 MIND YOUR OWN BUSINESS

- You call it: Heavenly Rewards
- You sell: Photos of loved ones as they are Raptured away
- You offer: Wallet-sized or suitable-for-framing. Multiple copies. Digital versions on DVD.

As the bodies begin to levitate, start taking pictures of the Rapturees — any and all of them, whoever is around you at the time, whether you know them personally or not. Take two or three shots per person and then move on; the idea is to photograph as many people as possible before they rise up out of range. If you can take video (and audio), do it. Put the photos on a Web site (be sure to protect them from being illegally copied), along with text advertising where and when they were taken. And don't worry about quality. These are the last pictures that will ever be taken of these people, and your customers won't be choosy. Create a PayPal account.

TAKE, AND SELL, STOCK

If you've taken our advice in the previous chapter and now have a big position in "godless-sector" holdings (gambling, liquor, et cetera), *bail out. Sell them all.* The Rapture, the most religious and godly event in our lifetime, will probably trigger an anti-godlessness backlash. We want you out of those industries before they tank.

FOR LATER ⏱

WATCHING YOUR INVESTMENTS GO SOUTH—AND LOVING IT!

If you've taken any of the above advice, you probably have accumulated a sizable amount of cash. What should you do with it? Easy.

Buy real estate!

The faithful Christians who will be Raptured to Heaven live all over the United States, of course, but it is no secret that the big majority of them reside in the American South. That's why, the day after the Rapture, we want you to get-on-down below the Mason-Dixon Line and start buying up homes, factories, and retail sites. It'll pay off big, for two reasons:

1. Out with the Godly, in with the Godless: After the Rapture, with the Christian faithful out of the picture, the South may prove to be very attractive to residents of New York or California seeking new areas in which to practice their godlessness without criticism or condemnation—and to get away from New York's and California's notoriously high real estate prices, property taxes, and congestion.

2. Instant Franchise: What kinds of buildings will be particularly available for sale and development after the Rapture? That's right: churches. They'll be perfect for "repurposing," e.g., for conversion into a chain of seafood places.

🐷 MIND YOUR OWN BUSINESS

- You call it: Holy Mackerel, Immortal Sole, Angel Fish, et cetera
- You sell: Virtuously nonmeat-based lunches and dinners
- You offer: Local fish and other seafood, regional specialties (to the new arrivals from New York and California!)

SHALOM, INVESTORS!

Buy Israel. Anything—construction company stocks, municipal bonds, land, investment property, the whole schmear. Why? See if you can guess:

a. Because it will make our parents happy.
b. Because Israel will have a growing economy, since few there will have been Raptured up.
c. Because the Antichrist will appear on the scene, make a seven-year covenant with Israel, and construction will begin on the Third Temple. (But more on that later.)

⚡ FEARFULLY ASKED QUESTIONS (FAQ) ⚡

Q. Isn't selling pictures of people's relatives being Raptured up rather intrusive and sacrilegious?
A. Not at all. You're offering private mementos of a public event. Think of it as being like taking photographs at the finish line of a marathon or at a senior prom.
Q. Am I allowed to buy real estate in Israel or invest in the rebuilding of the Third Temple if I am not Jewish?
A. Absolutely! Non-Jews are welcome and encouraged to invest in the Temple. You just can't belong to it.

Q. My best friend has just accepted Jesus as her personal savior, so I know that she will be Raptured up when the time comes. Is it too tacky if I ask her for her charm bracelet now?

A. Yes, it is. She is entitled to wear her charm bracelet, her dental fillings, and her prosthetic leg up until the very moment of the Rapture, at which point all of those items will be available for your use. But not before.

Part III The Tribulation: The Seal Judgments

CHAPTER 4

Meet the Antichrist

Have we got a guy for you!

> The Antichrist will be a man of enormous charm, dynamism, and charisma who will become the most popular political figure in the world. His coming is foretold by numerous passages in Scripture, including 1 John 2:18, 2 Thessalonians 2:3–4, and Matthew 24:24.

The Morning After . . .

If you read this book you'll wake up on the day after the Rapture knowing something that many people will not: The Antichrist is "out there" somewhere.

We don't know exactly where; he could be American, but some biblical interpretations suggest he will emerge from Eastern Europe. We're not sure if he'll be a strictly political figure or if he'll have pursued his career in some other field. But one thing we do know is that people all over the world will be absolutely crazy about him.

Sure, eventually he'll reveal his true plan, which is to kill millions of people and try to take over the world, and end up being inhabited by Satan, and then lead the largest army in history, representing Evil in its final, climactic fight against Good.

But that will come later. First he's going to unite the world and eliminate religious conflict and make his "brand" very, very big.

Naturally, you'll want "in" on this at the beginning. But there will be a problem: Of all the charismatic world-uniters running around after the Rapture, we won't know which specific one is the actual Antichrist.

Remember that whoever he is, he's not going to come forward and say, "Hi! I'm the Antichrist!" It's not even a title you can attain. It's not an office you can run for, like president, or a position you can be elevated to, like the pope. The term *Antichrist* is *negative*, so that's the last thing he'll call himself.

How, then, can we know which of the prominent political and cultural figures of our time is in fact the real Antichrist?

The Bible has foreseen this difficulty and has provided us with a wealth of clues, facts, and tips for identifying him. Whenever you spot a figure you think might qualify for the title Antichrist, compare his qualities and biographical details with this list:

The Antichrist . . .

Sits in the Tribulation Temple.
Claims to be God.
Has a mouth like a lion.
Causes men to worship Satan.
Requires his followers to be sealed on their foreheads
   or right hands.
Has blasphemous names.
Is married to a vile prostitute.
Is crowned with ten crowns.
Is called "the king."
Sits on a throne.
Has a bow in his hand.
Rides a white horse.

The Antichrist, somewhat resembling (per Scripture) the Cowardly Lion, shown here with his wife, the "Vile Prostitute." The Bible is silent on whether or not the couple has children.

Has an army.

Brings violent death.

Will ascend from the pit.

Will come in his own name.

Will exalt himself.

Will be admired.

Will be cast down to Hell.

Will come to do his own will.

Will come to destroy.

Is the "idol shepherd."

Is the "vine of the earth."

Is the "lie."

Is the "lawless one."

Is the "man of sin."

Is the "son of perdition."

Will be "the mystery of iniquity," i.e., Satan manifest in the flesh.

This is a pretty specific list, so it should be fairly easy to eliminate false candidates as they arise. Simply apply these criteria to whomever you suspect might be the Antichrist. For example:

✔ Michael Jackson may call himself "the King of Pop," which according to the above is pretty damning. But does Michael Jackson sit in the Tribulation Temple? Not to our knowledge.

✔ James Carville might, in some people's opinion, "be married to a vile prostitute," but does he "have a mouth like a lion"? Hardly.

✔ George W. Bush has indeed sat in "the Tribulation Temple" (or something equally grand) *and does* "claim to be (or at least converse with) God" *and* "have a mouth like a lion" (or at least speak English like one) *and* "require his followers to be sealed on their foreheads or right hands" ("You are either with us or against us") *and* "have blasphemous names" (for others, if not himself) *and* "be married to a vile prostitute" (or at least "a boring Stepford fem-bot with no discernible personality") *and* "have an army" *and* "ride a white horse" *and* "bring violent death." It's a pretty damning list. However, the whole world hates him, so he cannot be the Antichrist, whom the whole world will love and adore.

Remember that these descriptions are from the Bible. This means they're all true and they're all necessary. Meeting some or even most of these criteria doesn't count. Our pool man claims to be God; one of our nephews once wore ten cardboard crowns at a birthday party at Burger King; we know an actor who sits on a throne every year, in December, at the Glendale Galleria, pretending to be Santa Claus. But as far as we know, none of these figures is the Antichrist.

Jot down this list of twenty-eight requirements and keep it with you. Or better yet, commit it to memory. You'll never again have to wonder whether the person you've just met is the Antichrist.

Once you've found him, here's what to do.

⏱ FOR NOW

THE SHIRT ON YOUR BACK

When someone is famous, everyone just naturally wants to display his or her name and face on their clothing. That means that sooner or later, T-shirts with this guy's likeness, name, and logo are going hit *huge*. Why not make it happen for you?

🐖 MIND YOUR OWN BUSINESS

- You call it: An-TEE-Christ Industries
- You sell: Antichrist-branded merchandise
- You offer: T-shirts, bumper stickers, posters, sweatshirts, video games, action figures, bobble-head dolls, candy bars (Note: *Don't* call him "the Antichrist." [That designation will be our little secret.] Act fast and go in big, but beware of overcommitting and getting stuck with inventory. When, in a year or so, he reveals his Evil, his hotness will evaporate, the brand will go south, and you won't be able to give the stuff away.)

FLIP OUT!

Remember that real estate we told you to buy in the American South? One word: *sell*.

Three more words: SELL SELL SELL! Flip the houses! Unload the land! Find buyers for the shops and strip malls and buildings!

Why? Because your natural customer base for these holdings will, for reasons we explained earlier, include a lot of people from New York City and Southern California. And that means Jews. And very soon (see the next chapter) the Antichrist is going to rise to power and "do a deal" with Israel. As it so often does, the question becomes "Is it good for the Jews?" And the answer is "Yes, but . . ."

Overnight the Promised Land is going to become not only safe but a "hot" destination for émigrés from all over the world. That means that many American Jews who *would* have bought your southern real estate will decide instead to move to Israel—where, let's face it, unlike in the South, there's already a Jewish culture, and it's a dry heat. So bail out now. (And for "G-d's" sake, keep what you bought in Israel.)

FOR LATER ⏱

NEXT (FISCAL) YEAR IN JERUSALEM

Think about investing in the construction business in the city of Jerusalem: construction companies, concrete and cement companies, building materials, electrical and plumbing supplies, fine woodworking and metalworking studios, and so forth. Why? Pick one:

a. The Palestinian need for housing will result in a big condo boom.

b. Émigré Jews from LA will demand immediate construction of a Nordstrom and a Nate 'n Al deli.

c. The rebuilding of the Third Temple will mean a massive construction extravaganza.

FEARFULLY ASKED QUESTIONS (FAQ)

Q. Will I be required to pay a royalty to the Antichrist if I use his likeness on merchandise?

A. No. The Antichrist and his minions will be too busy craftily oppressing mankind to worry about commercial exploitation of his name and likeness. All he will ask is that you swear undying fealty to his rule or, failing that, suffer decapitation.

Q. Could the Antichrist somehow be prevented from being a bad man? Can he be saved before all the horrible stuff happens?

A. We're afraid not. All of this is destined to take place exactly as predicted. That's why we've written this book, and why we urge you to recommend it to your friends and loved ones. In addition, you (and they) might obtain benefit from our in-person lecture and seminar series ("Enriched, Enraptured, and Empowered!"), the DVD collection of the "best of" those lectures, our monthly Rapture-Tribulation ("Rap-Trib") newsletters ("Rap-Trib Rundown for Investors," "Rap-Trib Rundown for Savers," "Rap-Trib Rundown for Small Businesses," "Rap-Trib Rundown for Retirement," and "Rap-Trib Rundown for Kids"), and our next book, *Finding Love and Making It Work in the End Times*.

Q. I've always been attracted to "bad boys." Do you think I stand a chance with the Antichrist?

A. It's possible. But do you really want to? What kind of a relationship would that be? Do you really think that after a day of oppressing all of mankind, he'd take you out on a date and treat you nicely? Plus, bear in mind that about halfway into the Tribulation, he will be "indwelled" by Satan himself. Is that "bad" enough for you?

CHAPTER 5

The First Seal

The Antichrist Emerges

And So It Begins

> The Antichrist, in his capacity as world leader, will sign a seven-year "covenant," or peace treaty, with Israel. This will trigger the start of the seven-year Tribulation. It was foreseen in Daniel 9:27.

This is it. We're off and running. By now the Antichrist will have become head of a unified "one-world" government. When he signs this covenant, he will officially proclaim and guarantee Israel's legitimacy, security, and safety. And, since no one (except us) knows that he *is* the Antichrist, he'll be seen as some kind of miracle worker.

Israel, which until now has been a religious pressure cooker, embattled within and threatened from without, will overnight become *fabulous*. Tourism will go through the roof—which means investment in the country will take off. In fact, you may start to wonder: It's such a tiny country, what if there aren't enough things to invest *in*? Should you look for "spillover" opportunities in neighboring Egypt, Jordan, Syria, or Lebanon?

Not so fast! Of course, if you took our advice at the end of part II, you got in on the ground floor of this gigantic "Jew-boom" and are now sitting pretty. But even if you didn't, there will be plenty of other opportunities for you to go from a left-behind sinner to an out-in-front winner. Here are two.

🕐 FOR NOW

LAND OF LAND OF THE BIBLE LAND

As the whole world knows, industrious Israelis have "made the desert bloom," cultivating neglected, arid, lifeless terrain and converting it to lush, fertile farmland. But that was then, when the population was less than a million (in 1948) and you couldn't give away a four-day / three-night package. This is now, when millions of tourists will arrive hungry for the Holy Land experience—or at least for a safe, comfortable, Disneyland-like simulation of it. Someone is going to make a fortune acquiring a nice parcel of lush, fertile farmland and converting it *back* to neglected, arid, lifeless terrain—for the construction of Israelland (featuring "The Authentic Biblical Experience"), with rides ("Flight from Egypt Red Sea Water Slide"), exhibits ("Nazareth: Village of Contrasts"), and daily reenactments of classic Old and New Testament legends.

NEW FRIENDS, NEW ENEMIES

Learn, as quickly as possible, the home security business: burglar alarms, "safe rooms," intruder-detection systems, personal-protection gear, self-defense techniques, et cetera. Then get ready to travel to the tiny nation of Andorra, on the border between Spain and France.

Why?

When the Antichrist concludes his covenant with Israel, Muslims the world over will give up their anti-Jewish feelings. They'll fall in love with Israel and, shortly thereafter, with Jews. It will be great.

But it will also leave a "hate vacuum" in many authoritarian Middle Eastern countries. Rulers of Saudi Arabia, Iran, and Syria have survived for decades by uniting their otherwise angry, discontented populations against Israel (and her ally the United States). Once the Antichrist announces that Israel is "okay," whom will the radical Islamists next hate utterly and vow to destroy for all time?

We think it will be the Andorrans.

Not to be confused with Endora, who was Samantha's mother on *Bewitched,* Andorra is a tiny (181 square miles — it's 17 percent the size of Rhode Island) country located in the Pyrenees. We believe that radical Muslims everywhere will redirect their burning hatred from the Jews to all, or at least most, of the 72,000 people who live in Andorra.

Sure, this is about 22,000 fewer people than attended the Rose Bowl in 2006, so what kind of a threat can they be to anyone? Still, we have reached this conclusion for many reasons. For one thing, Andorra is a parliamentary democracy, which guarantees the kinds of freedoms that Islamic radicals supposedly just hate. Its main language is Catalan, which is an annoyingly marginal language to have to learn. It is home to folk dances like the *contrapás* and the *marratxa,* which radical Islamists probably can't stand. It's a tax haven, a tourist destination, and features what one Web site calls "the best skiing in the Pyrenees."

And, most offensive of all, the Andorran flag bears the images of *two cows.*

Islamic radicals will be provoked to a murderous frenzy by the cows on the Andorran flag. Traditional Islamic belief forbids the depiction of humans or animals in a religious context. Granted, a national flag isn't really a religious object. But it's close enough.

Add all these things together, and it's a wonder that radical Islamists have allowed Andorra to exist even this long. The tiny, soon-to-be-embattled nation will need help.

> ### 🐷 MIND YOUR OWN BUSINESS
>
> - You call it: Operation Enduring Andorra
> - You sell: Armed-response security teams, instruction
> - You offer: Home and small-business security equipment, instruction in the use of handguns and knives and various anti-attack sprays, martial arts instruction, and round-the-clock armed-response protection for residences and businesses

By the way, we have an alternative suggestion for exploiting Andorra's impending mortal danger, but it requires a huge outlay of capital that puts it beyond the budgets of most readers of this book. Still, for the sake of completeness, here it is:

Hire, equip, and train your own mercenary army. Then contract out your security/defense services to the Andorran government itself. Downside: large up-front cost in material and human resources. Upside: enormous "cost-plus" profits and an ability to operate in an atmosphere entirely free of legal restrictions (although the latter benefit will become increasingly available to everyone, everywhere in the days ahead).

Opening Day

The signing of the covenant with Israel may *technically* have begun the Tribulation, but with the opening of the First Seal, the End Times really shift into high gear.

With the signing of the covenant with Israel and the official commencement of the Tribulation, Jesus (often referred to as the

Lamb) will be handed a scroll with seven seals. (This will take place in Heaven.) As he opens the First Seal, a figure on a white horse will ride forth. This "White Horseman" symbolizes the Antichrist. His arrival in the world is foretold many times in Scripture, including in Daniel 11:36 and Revelation 6:1–2.

The rider on the white horse is the first of the famous Four Horsemen of the Apocalypse. Bear in mind that although there are seven seals, there are only four horsemen. The graph below depicts this fact in a more easily understood form.

NUMBER OF HORSEMEN PER SEAL

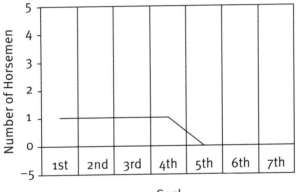

If you've decided to invest in An-TEE-Christ-brand T-shirts, bumper stickers, bobble-heads, and any other Antichrist-based personality items, be sure that you've done so by the opening of the First Seal. By then, the Antichrist's career will have really taken off. Once he unites all the nations of the Earth, the cat will be out of the bag.

Kickin' It Old Shul

The next major End Times event will be the reconstruction of a Jewish house of worship on the most contested piece of real estate in the world.

In order for several End Times prophecies to come true, the Third Temple in Jerusalem must be rebuilt on what the Israelis call the Temple Mount, in the heart of Jerusalem, where Abraham is said to have offered his son, Isaac, for sacrifice to God. It was there that the Second Temple was destroyed by the Romans in AD 70; on its site is also the Dome of the Rock, one of the holiest places in Islam, from which Muhammad is said to have ascended on a winged steed to Heaven. In addition, it is the site of the al-Aqsa mosque. In fact, it is the third-holiest site in all of Islam, after Mecca and Medina.

> The Third Temple of the Jews will be rebuilt on the Temple Mount to fulfill several predictions concerning the Antichrist, including Matthew 24:15–16, 2 Thessalonians 2:4, and Revelation 11:1–2.

The Third Temple will become the central place of worship for all of Judaism, where the Orthodox will resume sacrificing (and eating) sheep and bulls. Its rebuilding will require a massive undertaking both for its external shell and for its interior appointments. And that means loads of tempting financial opportunities!

🕐 FOR NOW

SUPPLIES AND DEMAND

Sure, once the Third Temple is built — you invested in those Israeli construction companies, didn't you? — you can get in on its supplies concessions, including:

* prayer books for daily services and High Holy Days
* Torahs
* "house" yarmulkes and tallit (prayer shawls)
* Torah covers, sashes, decorative metal plates, and yads (pointers)
* little triangular lightbulbs for the yahrzeit (commemoration) board
* office supplies
* shofars
* tzedakah (charity) boxes
* gift shop Judaica, including kiddush cups that look like they're from King Arthur and the Round Table, Seder plates that look like dartboards or mandalas, bulk-knit kippot (skullcaps), terra-cotta figurines and stuffed-toy replicas of the red heifer ritually sacrificed to purify the construction of the Temple, *Matisyahu Live in Tel Aviv Featuring Sly and Robbie* CDs, little models of the Temple itself, posters, "My Bubbie Went to the Third Temple and All I Got Was This Farkakteh T-Shirt" T-shirts, and mah-jongg mezuzah cases, mah-jongg pill cases, mah-jongg restaurant tip charts, mah-jongg menorahs, mah-jongg cell phone cases, mah-jongg umbrellas, mah-jongg magnifying glasses, mah-jongg change purses, mah-jongg handbags, and 20-piece melamine mah-jongg dinner sets

But everyone will probably think of this, so you may want to take a moment to think about the investment possibilities outside the building. Thousands, if not millions, of Jews from all over the world will conduct a pilgrimage — religious, cultural, or both — to the Temple. Isn't it obvious what they'll need? At any urban temple, parking is a big issue. This — the biggest synagogue in the world, in a tiny city with streets originally built for donkeys and camels — will be no exception.

🐷 MIND YOUR OWN BUSINESS

- You call it: Lot Parking ("Leave it here and don't look back.")
- You sell: Parking for all Temple activities
- You offer: Valet parking, while-you-pray car wash

And for after the service? For some reason, Jews—at least American Jews—love Chinese food. They even like Cantonese, which can be just as bland and ho-hum as Jewish cooking itself. When worshippers or tourists leave the Temple, they will be tired from all that travel and prayer, exultant at having made the pilgrimage to Israel—and hungry. The entrepreneur who opens a decent Chinese restaurant close to the Temple will make a killing. It probably won't even have to be kosher.

🐷 MIND YOUR OWN BUSINESS

- You call it: Temple Pagoda Temple
- You sell: Chinese food
- You offer: As wide a range as your chef and the available ingredients allow

The True False Prophet

The third and final big event connected with the opening of the First Seal is the emergence of the True False Prophet.

The False Prophet is the third part of the "Unholy Trinity" (along with the Antichrist and, of course, Satan). He will derive his power from the Antichrist and will, during the Tribulation, serve as the "high priest" of the Antichrist's religion. His coming is foretold in, among other places, Matthew 24:11 and Revelation 13:11–12 (*11: And I beheld another beast coming up out of the earth; and he had two horns like a lamb, and he spake as a dragon. 12: And he exerciseth all the power of the first beast before him, and causeth the earth and them which dwell therein to worship the first beast . . .*).

The False Prophet will be endowed (by Satan, via the Antichrist) with supernatural powers. He will, among other things, bring down fire from the heavens, and also create an "image" of the Antichrist that he will somehow endow with life. All this fulfills prophecies in Revelation 13:11–14.

As the Antichrist attempts to take over the entire world, the False Prophet will be his chief promoter. We think we know how he's going to raise money for his "boss," and we want you in on it.

🕐 FOR NOW

BONDS. ANTICHRIST BONDS

In 1997 rock singer David Bowie raised $55 million from the issue of ten-year asset-backed bonds, the collateral for which consisted of future royalties from twenty-five albums that he recorded before 1990. Other singing groups have followed suit, issuing what today are known as Pullman Bonds, after David Pullman, the banker who masterminded Bowie's groundbreaking deal.

How, we are often asked, is this possible?

The answer lies in the fact that people are very much like corporations. They can generate income just as corporations can. They can sue and be sued like corporations. They sell themselves in the labor market the way corporations sell their products in the marketplace. In fact, you can think of a human being as a kind of flesh-and-blood corporation.

All of this applies to the Antichrist, too. He'll need capital with which to advance his career—particularly if he is the figure mentioned in Scripture as the rider on the white horse, in which case he'll spend a lot of time riding all over the Earth, for which we assume he will not receive compensation.

That's why we expect some entity (under the direction of the False Prophet) to issue Pullman Bonds for the Antichrist. We recommend you consider them as part of your End Times portfolio. What you're investing in are the good deeds and *positive* things he will accomplish in the early stages of his career, before he becomes Evil incarnate—bringing peace to Israel, eliminating petty conflicts between nations, unifying the globe under his leadership, and so forth.

The collateral for the bonds will consist of the Antichrist's sheer charisma. During the two-year period following their issue, as he consolidates his power around the world, he should have no problem raising funds (via telethons and product endorsements) for making interest payments. At the conclusion of this period, he should easily be able to "call" the issue and pay off the face value of the bonds.

Bear in mind, however, that he might not. Once the Antichrist conquers the world, it's possible and even probable that he'll either default on interest payments or, alternatively, viciously murder all bondholders. That's why we constantly remind our readers that no investment is entirely without risk.

Still, if this kind of play interests you, be sure to purchase Antichrist and False Prophet bonds from reputable securities traders. We expect the issues to look something like this:

- **The All-Unity Non-Taxable Investment Coupon (or "Auntie-C")** will have a par of $1,000, a yield of 6 percent, and a maturity period of seven years. (Any longer maturity period is unfeasible, since in seven years the Antichrist will be thrown bodily into the Lake of Fire and will no longer be responsible for any debts public or private.)

☞ **The False Prophet Indeterminate Coupon ("F-Pick" or "Fal-Pro I-Coup")** will be offered with a par of $1,000 in a range of yields, from 1.25 percent to 6 percent, over a range of maturity periods. The longer the maturity, the higher the yield. The 6 percent issue will mature in seven years; the 1.25 percent bond will mature fifteen minutes after it is sold.

(NOTE: You may be tempted to buy and sell these bonds as you would a conventional investment vehicle. Buying is fine, but the Antichrist may interpret an attempt to sell them as demonstrating a lack of confidence in his plan for world domination. So our attorneys require us to print the following:
DISCLAIMER: Descriptions of Auntie-C's and F-Picks are in no way to be construed as recommendations for or against their purchase. Past performance is no guarantee of future results. Read prospectus carefully and then swear undying fealty to the Beast before investing. No guarantee that Antichrist and/or False Prophet will not oppress, persecute, smite, strike down, and/or slay investor attempting to sell above-mentioned securities is expressed or implied.)

FOR LATER 🕐

RADIO, WHISTLEBERRIES, AND SKIPPY TO TRAVEL
We suggest you put as much cash as you can afford into the purchase of canned tuna, canned beans, and peanut butter. Can you guess why?

a. To get in on the ground floor of a new "nonfresh" food craze.

b. As provisions for an epic covered-wagon journey across the United States.

c. To prepare for an imminent worldwide famine.

🗲 FEARFULLY ASKED QUESTIONS (FAQ) 🗲

Q. I'm thirty-four years old and I plan to retire at age sixty. Should I get F-Pick long-terms and roll them over every seven years, or will I get eaten alive by the tax man?

A. Retire at sixty? You'll be lucky to be alive at forty-one. In seven years the world will end. This means it's not the tax man you have to worry about. It's the Lord of Hosts, who in His implacable wrath will visit judgment upon a sinful world. That said, we like the seven-year Auntie-C's for their slightly better Moody's rating.

Q. Covenant or no covenant, it's hard to imagine the world's billion Muslims agreeing to let the Jews, assisted by the Christians, treat the al-Aqsa mosque and the Dome of the Rock as a "tear down." Why should I invest in the Third Temple's construction when it can't possibly be rebuilt?

A. It does sound improbable, but remember, all this will happen at the behest of the Antichrist, whom people will love and adore and just not be able to say no to.

Q. If I buy Auntie-C bonds, aren't I in effect helping the Antichrist in his evil deeds? Isn't that bad? Won't I go to Hell?

A. It is bad, and if that's all you do, you will indeed go not to Hell but into the Lake of Fire, which is at a separate location. But you can prevent that by, at any time during the Tribulation, accepting Jesus as your personal savior — an act that will neutralize and render moot anything else you may have done, including investing in the activities of the Antichrist.

CHAPTER 6

The Second Seal

War

The Honeymoon Is Over

The Opening of the Second Seal is going to make the Opening of the First Seal seem like the opening of a Bed Bath and Beyond. War is unleashed, and the Antichrist reveals his true nature.

> When Jesus opens the Second Seal it will cue the Red Horseman, who represents war, as disclosed in Revelation 6:3–4.
>
> This war will be fairly "low-tech." Rather than by conventional armies using rifles, planes, bombs, tanks, and missiles, these battles will be fought by *"a great company with bucklers and shields, all of them handling swords,"* as noted in Ezekiel 38:4.

The first question is, what are bucklers? They're shields you wear on your body, like big belts. Shields, then, are the things you hold in your hand, and swords, of course, are swords.

The second question is, why will this war be fought with such primitive equipment, when most countries already have a broad array of modern armaments, from AK-47s to atomic bombs, and ordinary "street punks" walk around major US cities with semi-automatic weapons? The answer, of course, is that the Bible says so—but it's easy to see why. With everyone going broke paying the high cost of gasoline, it's only a matter of time before the nations of the world move away from fossil fuel–based weapons and toward more "green" methods of waging war.

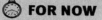 **FOR NOW**

EN GARDE — FOR PROFIT!

To profit from the War of the Second Seal, forget investing in Lockheed Martin, Halliburton, Northrup Grumman, Boeing, or any of the other usual defense companies in the military-industrial complex. This war will be conducted by men on horseback stabbing one another.

The table on the next page lists the typical kinds of equipment whose providers you'd invest in under normal circumstances of armed conflict, and the supplies that will replace them for the low-tech War of the Second Seal.

Get the picture? We don't even think they'll use styptic pencils. Put your money into companies that make swords and shields, and maybe horses and riding equipment. Period.

I'm Thinking of a Number Between 665 and 667

Having won the War of the Second Seal, the Antichrist will keep going—and the False Prophet will come up with a marketing brainstorm.

> The Antichrist will be victorious in the sword-fought war and, with the help of the False Prophet, advance his conquest of the entire world. The False Prophet will issue an edict commanding all people to take the "mark" of the Antichrist, i.e., to inscribe the famous and mysterious number 666 on their foreheads

COMPARISON OF CONVENTIONAL VS. SECOND SEAL WEAPONS AND MATÉRIEL

Purpose	High-Tech, Conventional Military Equipment (US Army, 2007)	Low-Tech, Second Seal Counterpart
Body protection	Joint Service Lightweight Integrated Suit Technology	Bucklers
Face, head protection	M40-42 series field protective masks	Small and large shields, helmets
Ordnance	M-4 carbines, M-9 pistols, M-16 rifles, MK 19-3 grenade machine guns, M203 grenade launchers, M-240B machine guns, M-249 squad automatic weapons, MLRS's, M102 towed howitzers, M119 towed howitzers, M198 towed howitzers, M120/M121 mortars, M224 mortars, M252 mortars, Paladins, Javelins, Phased Array Tracking Intercept of Target (PATRIOT) missiles, TOW missile systems, Avenger Stinger missile launch pods, bayonets	Swords, bows and arrows, war clubs, spears, slings, knives, rocks, sticks, fists, feet
Transport	Heavy expanded-mobility tactical trucks, high-mobility multipurpose wheeled vehicles, M1070 heavy equipment transporters, Stryker vehicles, Apache Longbow helicopters, Kiowa Warrior helicopters, Abrams tanks, Bradley fighting vehicles, M88A2 Hercules tanks	Horses, saddles, bridles, reins, stirrups
Food	Meals Ready to Eat (MRE's)	Looted villages, plundered crops, dead horses
Fuel	Gasoline, diesel, kerosene, electricity, batteries	Hay, oats, grass
Stimulants	Vitamins, steroids, Ecstasy, amphetamines, cocaine, marijuana, beer	Wine, strong drink
Medicine, medical equipment	Antibiotics, disinfectants, surgical supplies, analgesics, tranquilizers, splints, stretchers, plasma, IV's, bronchoscopes, defibrillators, gauze, prostheses	Rag bandages, rope tourniquets

or right hands. Many of those who refuse will face execution, principally by beheading. Those who don't have the Mark of the Beast® but are not executed will be *forbidden to buy or sell.*

This is famously foretold in Revelation 13:16–18 (*16: And he causeth all, both small and great, rich and poor, free and bond, to receive a mark in their right hand, or in their foreheads. 17: And that no man might buy or sell, save he that had the mark, or the name of the beast, or the number of his name. 18: Here is wisdom. Let him that hath understanding count the number of the beast: for it is the number of a man; and his number is Six hundred threescore and six*).

The Antichrist will seek to establish his trademark ("666") and extend his "brand" to every living person by requiring each individual to wear the symbol on his or her right hand or forehead. Anyone who fails to display the Mark® faces one of two equally monstrous fates.

One is decapitation. The other is that the victim will be forbidden to buy or sell stocks or bonds. In fact, this is the only biblical injunction we know of that explicitly deals with the securities markets.

There are some scholars who interpret the scriptural passage to mean that anyone not taking the Antichrist's Mark® will be forbidden to buy or sell *anything,* such as food or clothing. But we think that's just unrealistic. Who can live like that? Believe us, not being allowed to make trades in the market is bad enough— especially if you're sitting on a portfolio that's gone up and you're looking to take profits. To be barred from selling those shares is our idea of hell on earth. And it should be yours, too!

Once this edict is issued, there will be three kinds of people in the world: those who agree to display the Antichrist's Mark®, those who decline his actual Mark® but attempt to wear a simulation of it, and those who refuse to wear his Mark® in any fashion. We will refer to these three types as the Take Its, the Fake Its, and the Forsake Its. Each has its own values and motivations. Which one are you?

1. **The Take Its**: Some of these people will take the Antichrist's Mark® because they're terrified of him and of the penalties he will impose on those who refuse. This response is perfectly understandable, since many people view with horror the possibility of having their heads chopped off or of being forbidden to trade stocks or bonds. Others will be people who still, in spite of everything, believe that the Antichrist is the greatest, most charismatic guy in the whole wide world.

2. **The Fake Its**: These people know, via the Bible, that those who accept the actual 666® of the Antichrist will ultimately be cast for eternity into the Lake of Fire by an angry, indignant God. But they will be unwilling to openly defy the Antichrist and risk death or exile from Wall Street. They will therefore contrive to wear a fake Mark® in an effort to fool the Antichrist's inspectors or agents, while inwardly rejecting him. No one knows whether God will "buy" this or not.

3. **The Forsake Its**: These are the people who refuse to wear the Evil One's Mark® for any reason and in any form—some for the sake of their eternal souls, and others because they disapprove of tattoos or just don't like being told what to do. They will knowingly run the risk of execution or of not being able to invest in securities.

Once the Antichrist issues his order, the question of whether to Take It, Fake It, or Forsake It will dominate people's thoughts and conversations the world over—including, possibly, yours.

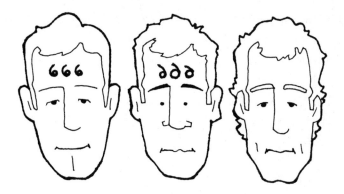

The three ways of dealing with the Antichrist's Mark®. Note telltale
homemade nature of "Fake It" mark (center).

DECISIONS, DECISIONS

The arguments in favor of taking the Antichrist's Mark® are persuasive, but so are the arguments against it. Many people will therefore find themselves stymied by doubt and second thoughts. That's why we're offering, free of charge to readers of this book, a basic introductory version of our Mark® Metric Preference Index (MMPI).

This scientifically designed personality profile has been created to help the user understand his or her deepest needs, fears, and desires with regard to having someone tattoo 666 on him or her. The test below consists of twenty yes-or-no questions. From this we can get a rough idea of whether you should be a Take It, a Fake It, or a Forsake It.

But remember, twenty questions is just a beginning. For a more detailed, accurate, and comprehensive profile, we encourage you to take the full test of all 573 questions. The fee for this is normally $19.95, with family and AAA discounts available. However, a $10 rebate is available upon submission (via fax or mail) of proof of purchase of this book, resulting in a final cost of only $9.95. And, if you act now, before the Tribulation begins, you can take advantage of our special "Pre-Trib" Earlybird Rate and save an additional four dollars. That's the *complete test* for only $5.95.

For starters, though, take the introductory test, below, with our compliments.

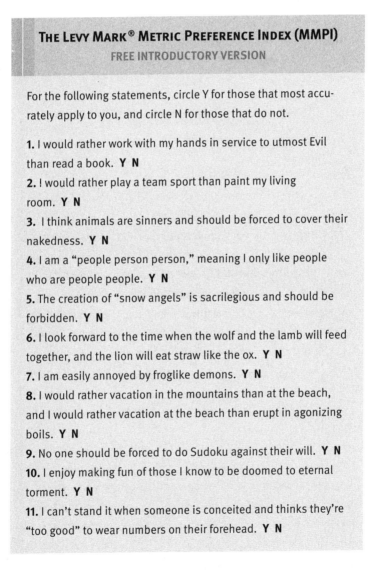

THE LEVY MARK® METRIC PREFERENCE INDEX (MMPI)
FREE INTRODUCTORY VERSION

For the following statements, circle Y for those that most accurately apply to you, and circle N for those that do not.

1. I would rather work with my hands in service to utmost Evil than read a book. **Y N**

2. I would rather play a team sport than paint my living room. **Y N**

3. I think animals are sinners and should be forced to cover their nakedness. **Y N**

4. I am a "people person person," meaning I only like people who are people people. **Y N**

5. The creation of "snow angels" is sacrilegious and should be forbidden. **Y N**

6. I look forward to the time when the wolf and the lamb will feed together, and the lion will eat straw like the ox. **Y N**

7. I am easily annoyed by froglike demons. **Y N**

8. I would rather vacation in the mountains than at the beach, and I would rather vacation at the beach than erupt in agonizing boils. **Y N**

9. No one should be forced to do Sudoku against their will. **Y N**

10. I enjoy making fun of those I know to be doomed to eternal torment. **Y N**

11. I can't stand it when someone is conceited and thinks they're "too good" to wear numbers on their forehead. **Y N**

12. Satan is misunderstood and the victim of "bad publicity." **Y N**

13. I am frequently jealous of celebrities. **Y N**

14. I would rather sing praises to God in an eternal state of ecstasy than be thrown into the Lake of Fire. **Y N**

15. People who eat ketchup on hot dogs should be shot. **Y N**

16. I find wool clothing to be itchy and uncomfortable. **Y N**

17. People who jog are trying to run away from salvation. **Y N**

18. Just because someone is glamorous and charismatic doesn't mean he's the Antichrist. **Y N**

19. I enjoy arguing about the importance of public transportation. **Y N**

20. Most people are horrible. **Y N**

YOUR SCORE

Count the number of yes answers you gave, then consult this scale:

IF YOU SCORED **1–7** YES ANSWERS, you are a Forsake It. You should refuse to take the Antichrist's Mark®. You have a strong sense of self, and your integrity means the world to you. You are a positive and hopeful person, which sometimes, like now, will not serve you — but at least you can look at yourself in the mirror and like who you see. You're a big-time romantic. You believe good guys finish first and tend to wear pastels and drive Hondas or Toyotas. You are true and honest right up till the end, which, sadly, will be soon.

IF YOU SCORED **8–14** YES ANSWERS, you are a Fake It. You should *pretend* to take the Mark® of the Antichrist but not really mean it. You enjoy, and even thrive on, high-risk investments and extreme sports. You work hard and play harder. You live life on the edge because that's where you're most comfortable. "Security"? Forget it. Security is for old people and losers. What's the point of having a heart if it's not in your mouth? Your color is red; your car is not (as one might think) the Porsche or the Lamborghini, but rather a 1972 Datsun whose gears keep slipping and whose brakes could give out at any moment. You love life and are not afraid of death. In fact, you dare death to come and find you. You taunt death. One day death will taunt back, but for now: Go for it.

IF YOU SCORED **15–20** YES ANSWERS, you are a Take It. You should absolutely take the Antichrist's Mark®. The idea of not being able to buy or sell stocks and bonds is a fate worse than death for you. It's not that you're evil; you're just too busy making money to judge what others do in their spare time. You live in a condo rather than a house because you don't care about lawns. The only green thing you like is money. Your favorite mode of transportation is the ladder of success. Your idea of a vacation is working from home. Sure, by taking the Mark® you will drink of the wine of God's fury, which has been poured full strength into the cup of His wrath, and you will be tormented with burning sulfur in the presence of the holy angels and the Lamb, and the smoke of your torment will rise forever and ever. So what? No pain, no gain!

🕐 FOR NOW

NO-TELL MOTEL

People who refuse the Mark of the Beast® will, by necessity, become fugitives. They will be forced to move from town to town, from one hiding place to another, to avoid capture and punishment by the Antichrist's minions. Where will they spend the night?

We have a solution to this problem that just might be the kind of thing you're looking for to provide a handsome revenue stream.

We call it Motel 666 — an inn catering to a particular niche market of travelers, including those on a budget, those in need of short-term residences, and those in flight from being beheaded. Its main selling point, especially to those running away from the Antichrist, is that it will be decorated *in a pro-Antichrist motif.*

Its distinctive features will include:

✔ **No Gideon Bibles.** Instead, each nightstand contains a copy of either *The Satanic Rituals,* by Anton Szandor LaVey, *The Annotated Playboy Philosophy,* by Hugh M. Hefner, or *Why I Am Not a Christian,* by Bertrand Russell.

✔ **No phone books or Yellow Pages, with their listings of area churches.** Instead, each room will be equipped with a copy of the latest edition of the "fully illustrated" Pleasure Toy World and Hot Thong International Mail Order Catalog.

✔ They say cleanliness is next to godliness. That's why all Motel 666 rooms feature **badly running water, not enough hot water, ratty carpets,** and **no soap.** Also, usually, **unwashed linens from previous guests.**

✔ Complimentary continental breakfast featuring **vodka, pain-killers,** and **cheap cigarettes**

✔ **Coed naked sauna**

✔ **Coed naked swimming pool**

✔ **Coed naked coffee shop**

✔ **Coed naked gift shop**

✔ **Coed naked "business center"**

✔ **Coed naked lobby**

✔ **X-rated (and nothing else) cable TV**

✔ **One-button direct-dial line to out-call "escort" service**

✔ **Unsavory night manager who probably deals drugs**

Yes, it sounds disgusting, repellent, and downright evil—and that's the point. No henchman for the Antichrist would think of looking in such a place for a person who refused the Mark®. (Although they might want to stay there—keep your eyes peeled!) Plus we think you'll get a lot of "tourist" guests just seeking to satisfy their curiosity.

Whether you open a single Motel 666 or acquire financing and open a chain, you'll be doing well by doing good by appearing to be doing bad. And that's a good feeling.

FOR LATER ⏱

WHAT GOES UP . . .

The Antichrist has conquered the world. His bond issues, the Auntie-C's and the F-Picks, are in demand. What should you do?

"Short" them.

"Shorting," or "selling short," is the opposite of normal securities trading. Customarily, you buy a security, wait for its price to go up, and then sell. Shorting, however, is a play to make when you think the price of a security is going to go down.

Here's how it works: Your broker borrows shares from someone who owns them, promising to replace them. (You'll need a margin account with your broker.) The broker gives them to you, and you immediately sell them. If/when the stock goes down, you "cover the short position" by buying them back at the lower price. You return the shares, pay the broker expenses and commission, and keep the rest.

Of course, the stock could go up—indefinitely—and sooner or later you'd have to buy back the shares in order to return them. Your potential losses, therefore, are infinite. That's why short-selling is recommended for only the most sophisticated traders.

But you can take it from us (and from the book of Revelation):

Pretty soon the Antichrist's "stock" *is* going to go down. *Hard.* So find a broker, borrow some Auntie-C's, and sell them. Then hang on until the next chapter. Just don't let the Antichrist know that you're betting against him.

IMPORTANT NOTE: SECURITIES TRADING FOR FORSAKE ITS

If you're a Forsake It, you've been forbidden to buy or sell any security. So, from here on out, when we advise you to trade stocks or bonds, you'll have to employ the services of an intermediary. He or she can be a broker, of course, but the accounts will have to be in the broker's name or in a fictitious name to which the broker has access. And, of course, the broker will have to be someone who has taken the Antichrist's Mark®. Look for securities dealers who are "Antichrist authorized," "666 certified," et cetera.

PREPARING FOR A NON-RAINY DAY

If you've taken our previous advice, you've had some experience investing in Israeli companies. Now is a good time to put money (via an intermediary if necessary; see above) into companies—either in Israel or those who have markets there—in hydroponics (growing fruits and vegetables in water), agrichemicals, and vitamins. Why?

a. Because Israelis will have become too fat and will be looking to high-chemical diets and supplements to slim down.
b. Because Israel will initiate a program to send people into outer space, and this is what the "spaceschleppers" will eat.
c. Because a severe drought will afflict Israel, starting very soon.

FEARFULLY ASKED QUESTIONS (FAQ)

Q. Rather than shorting Auntie-C's, wouldn't it be smarter to buy put options on them? Especially since you claim to know the time period in which their value is going to plummet?

A. No. Put options are a way of hedging your bet that the price of the bond will go down. This means your return is lower. Take our word for it: The price of Auntie-C's is going to go down, period. Stick with shorting and leave the puts to the fancy-pants day traders who will wake up one day with their heads in a basket.

Q. I love the idea of opening a motel — I've always wanted to run my own B&B. Do you think, aside from those fleeing the Antichrist, there will be a big tourist boom around the United States?

A. No, but we think there will be a big chaos, dislocation, and anarchy boom, which is like a tourist boom, except conducted in a spirit of panic and terror instead of leisure and fun.

Q. Help! I took the MMPI test three different times and came up with three different personality profiles. So should I take the Antichrist's Mark® or not?

A. You might try to "split the difference." Instead of taking the full 666 Mark®, try taking just one 6. Or maybe 66.6. God will probably find out in the end, but maybe He'll give you a break.

CHAPTER 7

The Third Seal

Famine

Feeling Peckish

The opening of the Third Seal brings good news and bad news. The good news is that the war is over. The bad news is that there's nothing to eat.

> In Heaven, Jesus will open the Third Seal, cueing the Black Horseman, who will bring famine into the world. This will fulfill not only the prophecy in Matthew 24:7 but more explicitly that of Revelation 6:5–6.

Real Home "Cooking"

Remember when, in chapter 2 of this section, we told you to run out and by a ton of tuna and peanut butter and beans? Now we'll tell you why: The Third Seal has been opened, and famine has been ushered into the world.

In a moment we're going to show you how to barter your surplus food for useful everyday items, including other food. You can, of course, sell your extra supply for money, too. But in times of famine, money isn't the problem.

In fact, it's possible that you'll have a hard time actually finding other food to barter for *or* buy, since the Third Horseman will be riding around destroying it all. You may be stuck eating a lot of tuna, beans, and peanut butter. That's why we've included, below, several mouthwatering recipes to demonstrate how, with just a little creativity, these three basic ingredients can take you pretty far. Let the recipes serve as a springboard to spark your imagination to create others. Tip: To cut down on having to cook all week, simply triple all ingredient amounts. Each recipe can then be re-served over two to three days.

NOTE: All recipes call for creamy peanut butter and tuna packed in water unless otherwise indicated.

Tuna "Satay" with Bean Compote

SERVES 2

1 can tuna
½ cup peanut butter
1 can pinto, kidney, or other beans

1. Open can, drain tuna.
2. Place peanut butter in small bowl.
3. Add tuna to peanut butter. Mix. Set aside, allowing flavors to "marry."
4. In a medium saucepan over moderate heat, simmer beans, in their liquid, until tender, about 20 minutes.
5. With potato masher, fork, or meat mallet, mash beans coarsely. Be careful not to over-mash.
6. Serve tuna–peanut butter "satay" on plate along with portion of bean compote.

Tuna-Bean "Surprise" in Peanut Sauce

SERVES 2

1 can beans
1 can tuna
½ cup peanut butter
1 cup water

1. Open, drain can of beans. Reserve bean liquid. Pour beans onto plate.
2. Working quickly, split each bean lengthwise and scoop out flesh. Reserve flesh.
3. Open, drain can of tuna. Pour onto plate.
4. Using two forks, shred tuna into tiny slivers.
5. Place one or two slivers of tuna into each hollowed-out bean "shell." Seal "shells" by rubbing seam gently until sealed.
6. Over low heat, heat re-sealed beans in 1 cup water until warmed through.
7. While beans are warming, make the sauce: Place reserved bean liquid and bean flesh in food processor. Pulse several times to blend. Add peanut butter in small amounts, pulsing until thoroughly blended.
8. Pour small portion of sauce onto plate, top with beans, serve. Pass rest of sauce.

Mock Nigerian "Groundnut Stew" with Fish Appetizer

SERVES 2

1 cup peanut butter
1 can beans
1 can tuna

1. Place peanut butter in saucepan.
2. Open beans. Add beans, with liquid, to peanut butter.

3. Stir well. Cook over medium heat until peanut butter is melted and beans are heated through.
4. While "stew" is cooking, make fish appetizer: Open, drain tuna. Place on plate.
5. Serve fish appetizer first, followed by "stew."

And, if you like to cook, bear this in mind: People all over the country are going to be increasingly "on the move" and will be too busy to make their own meals. By preparing the above recipes in large quantities, you can turn a nice profit selling these dishes to a clientele literally starving for something "fresh."

🐷 MIND YOUR OWN BUSINESS

- You call it: Trio: An Experience of Eating Food
- You sell: The above three tuna / bean / peanut butter dishes, plus any others you can create
- You offer: Hot, reasonably freshly made meals complete with protein (the tuna, the peanut butter, the beans) and fiber (the beans) to travelers, refugees from the Antichrist, refugees from the war, refugees from the famine

And, of course, these ingredients combine well with others, such as salt. Use some of your profits to expand your menu by featuring a weekly "String Bean Day" or "Pickled Beet Festival."

Legal, Tender

Most people can understand how in times of famine, food acquires "value" that can equal and even exceed that of actual money. When you or your loved ones are starving, a fifty-dollar bill is just a piece of paper, and you'd gladly trade it for a couple corned beefs on rye.

Because this kind of crisis will be widespread thanks to the Third Seal, food will become as coveted as dollars. Transferable units of food will become an informal medium of exchange. That makes your stockpiled canned goods all the more valuable.

But how do you calculate the value of one bartered item for another? How do you convert Yukon Gold potatoes into dandruff shampoo? Mankind has been asking this question for thousands of years, and we're going to have to resume asking it all over again.

To get you started, we've calculated just how much various common, in-demand items cost, as expressed in six-ounce cans of chunk light tuna (@ $.89 in 2008 dollars). We've done the math for converting tuna into a can of "store brand" pinto beans, a "salon-style" haircut, a (new) thirty-inch Kenmore free-standing self-cleaning electric range, and a (used) 2002 Nissan Maxima SE sedan, with six-speed manual transmission, air-conditioning, power steering, CD/cassette/FM, ABS, rear spoiler, and alloy wheels, with 60,000 miles and in "excellent" condition.

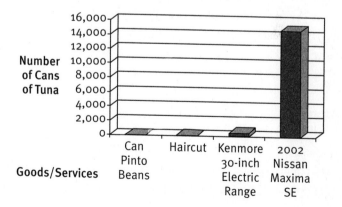

COMMONLY BARTERED GOODS EXPRESSED AS SIX-OUNCE CANS OF CHUNK LIGHT TUNA

The results are on the graph above. Use them as the basis for other calculations of your own.

(NOTE: You may not be in the market for an electric range, which will grow less useful as the Tribulation proceeds. But you may already have one to sell or trade. As the chart suggests, for such "big-ticket" items, cans of tuna and cans of beans are effectively interchangeable. Your goal in all such trading should be to get as many beans as you can.)

Gone Today, Here Tomorrow

One of the most electrifying events connected with the opening of the Third Seal will take place when the Antichrist is attacked. Will he die?

> Somehow—it is not clear where or why—the Antichrist will appear to have died. Then, after being seen to be dead, he will return to life. All of this is set forth in Revelation 13:3–4.

The Antichrist's death and resurrection will understandably cause a sensation around the world, and will solidify his stature as the greatest ruler on Earth. It may take place in Assyria—whatever *that* means, since Assyria was an ancient kingdom the area of which today includes portions of Egypt, Israel, Jordan, Iraq, Syria, Saudi Arabia, and Turkey, so good luck finding it. Who will kill him and how the killer will be able to do it (possibly with "a sword") are unknown.

What is known, however, is that his return to life will probably take place courtesy of Satan, who will have just been kicked out of Heaven after losing a war with the Archangel Michael. Satan will fall to Earth, where he will "indwell" the Antichrist, literally occupying his body and equipping him with his own supernatural powers. If this were a movie it would be "the ultimate buddy picture" meets "bad cop/worse cop."

⏱ FOR NOW

BUY BUY, BABY, BUY BUY

Earlier we told you to "short" Auntie-C and F-Pick bonds. If you did, you borrowed shares, sold them, and you're sitting on the cash those sales generated. Now you'll see what we had in mind. At the news of the Antichrist's "death" the market will *absolutely tank*. His bonds will go down the tubes. When this happens, and everyone thinks that this beloved world leader has died, we have one word for you:

Buy! (Again: If you're a Forsake It, do it discreetly, through a third party. But do it!)

Buy those bonds! Buy them like crazy! Buy with cash, on margin, or with cans of smoked oysters. Just buy!

Start by "covering your short position," which simply means buying enough shares to return the ones you borrowed earlier. Because you sold the borrowed ones when they were high and are now buying them back at a lower price, you've made a profit on that group of shares.

But don't stop there! Keep buying! And be sure to do it *immediately* after the Antichrist's (supposed) death. Yes, everyone you know will be selling, and your broker will balk at it, and you'll feel a little weird. Just do it.

Why? Because although the world "knows" the Antichrist is dead, *it doesn't know he's about to come back to life.* Whereas you do.

But you've got to act during the interval between his death and his resurrection. And we just don't know how long that will be. Jesus had what, before he was resurrected—three days? That was God's idea of a fast turnaround. We're dealing now with Satan, who could move much faster. The Bible is, uncharacteristically, not very helpful on this point. But that interval will form the "window" of time in which you must buy Auntie-C's and F-Picks. We estimate it to be between twenty minutes and an entire day—just long enough for the world to hear about his death (and start dumping his bonds).

HE, THE LIVING

When the Antichrist returns from the dead, what do you think will happen? That's right: The market will *soar*. For those who admire him, his return will mark the most spectacular career comeback in history. And even for those who hate his guts, it will signal the reestablishment of order and stability (which are two things the markets like even more than charisma), and the mitigation of uncertainty and confusion (which the markets hate even more than Absolute Evil).

So when word arrives that the Antichrist is alive, play it cool. Let Auntie-C's and F-Picks go up for a few days. Then, when it looks like they've leveled off, sell.

MOVING ON . . .

If you own your home at the time the Antichrist comes back to life, we urge you to sell it as quickly as you can. Things are going to get increasingly hectic and distressing now that the Antichrist is indwelled by Satan. You're going to want to be as mobile and "liquid" as possible. If it makes you feel any better, bear in mind that by now there are only three and a half years until the Second Coming, at which point "owning your own home" will be the last thing anyone cares about—even with the mortgage interest tax deduction. *That's* how "big" the Second Coming is going to be.

Two Guys from Heaven Walk into a Bar . . .

Sometime after the Third Seal is opened, God will send down two supernatural witnesses to Jerusalem. Although their identities are the subject of dispute, most agree that one will be the Jewish prophet Elijah; the other will probably be Moses. The Two Witnesses will have the power to send fire out of their mouths (as Elijah did once already, in the Old Testament). They will also be able to "shut up the heavens," bringing drought, most likely to the Middle East. And they will have the ability to turn rivers, lakes, et cetera into blood (as Moses did when he brought the plagues to Egypt). All of this is predicted in Revelation 11:3–6.

The task of the Two Witnesses will be to counteract the lies of the Antichrist and to exhort the Jews to accept Jesus as Savior. But it won't work. Israel will essentially remain in unbelief until the time of her greatest persecution, the Day of God's Wrath in the second half of the Tribulation.

One of the interesting points about the Two Witnesses is that even though (a) they're Elijah and, probably, Moses, and (b) they can emit fire from their mouths, people will still refuse to believe they are anything special or important.

Weird? Not necessarily.

For one thing, by this time emitting fire from your mouth will be seen to be "no big deal," since the False Prophet is able to do it. Also, we think people will dismiss the witnesses' ancient appearance and their bossy, moralistic nagging as being "OT" (meaning "unattractively or objectionably Old Testament") in the way some people reject certain things today as being "PC."

Indeed, most people will consider the Two Witnesses to be just a couple of religious "nuts," false prophets running around the Holy Land, chastising the Jews and calling on them to accept Christ (which, as Jews, they can't do), and making everyone feel either bad or embarrassed, like the Jews for Jesus you see at airports.

Which doesn't mean, of course, that they can't be marketed.

⏱ FOR NOW

MO AND EJ: KEEPIN' IT ANCIENT

Paradoxically, the one group we think will find the Two Witnesses perversely appealing is teenagers. High school and college kids, who are always eager to offend and defy their parents in matters of style, will immediately adopt the "fashion backward" look of Elijah and Moses. (See below for an artist's conception of how contemporary teens will put their unique "spin" on the witnesses' ultra-traditional robe-and-sandals motif.)

M-MAN AND E-JAH

Call us crazy, but we think that the Two Witnesses, with their hectoring, moralistic evangelizing and their colorful manner of

Teens influenced by "old-school" style of Elijah and, probably, Moses. Despite biblical source, parents will still "not get" why kids dress the way they do.

speech, would make a great pair of action heroes. Not to mention the fact that they possess superpowers and they *arrive* wearing capes, sort of.

Hollywood is always desperate to make blockbuster movies as safely as possible, about familiar characters. Well, is there a more familiar character in history than Moses? Elijah, admittedly, is less known to non-Jews, but even so, he's a natural to play Moses's "sidekick." It's easy to imagine them squabbling and wisecracking in Bible-ese as they vanquish bad guys and fight crime, all the while being misunderstood by their fellow Jerusalemites.

Therefore, as soon as you learn of the witnesses' arrival in Israel, find their agent and look into creating some sort of partnership exploiting their names, characters, and likenesses.

Just don't let the project languish in "development hell" for too long. The Two Witnesses are going to remain on Earth for only three and a half years—and that's three and a half literal, traditional years, since in this book we only apply "biblical math" (multiplying something times 360) to the Rapture itself. That's not a lot of time in which to get the movie made, especially if Elijah and Moses have final script approval. Which they will, if their representation is any good.

FOR LATER ⏱

While the world is relaxing after the Antichrist's miraculous return from death, we want you to drop everything, get on the phone, and do this:

Sell all your Israel-based stock.

And we mean *all* of it: in construction companies, tourism, agriculture, whatever. Whether it's been up or down lately, sell it. Why? Because something bad is going to happen to Israel very soon, and we want you out of there before it does.

Oh, and the Antichrist is going to demand that the entire world call him by a different title. Can you guess what it is?

a. Mister Antichrist
b. The King of Swing
c. God

⚡ FEARFULLY ASKED QUESTIONS (FAQ) ⚡

Q. How do we know that this whole famine thing isn't God's way of telling us we're all too fat?

A. We know because nowhere does it say in the Bible that we will be too fat in God's eyes and that He will punish us with famine.

Q. Why do Elijah and Moses, who originally were Jews, change their minds about Jesus being the Messiah?

A. They don't. Remember that they lived before Jesus was born, and so they had no opportunity to have an opinion one way or the other about Him. Since their original deaths they have been in Heaven, where they presumably met Jesus and got to know Him and decided He is the Messiah.

Q. Are Elijah and Moses gay? If not, why are they "paired up"?

A. As far as we know, they are not gay. Moses, as you know, was married to Zipporah for around eighty or ninety years. Now, it's true that being married doesn't mean you're not gay, but there is no scriptural evidence that either Moses or Elijah was anything but straight. Rather, they are "paired up" because, as the Two Witnesses, they are subjected to many dangers. This way, if one of them is in trouble, the other can go for help. Plus, as a team they can trade wisecracks to keep their morale high.

CHAPTER 8

The Fourth Seal
Death

Almost Halftime

Congratulations! We're almost halfway through the seven years of the entire Tribulation! If everything is going as it should, it's time for Death.

> When Jesus opens the Fourth Seal, He will unleash the final Horseman of the Apocalypse, Death. This is foretold in Revelation 6:7–8 (*8: And I looked, and behold a pale horse: and his name that sat on him was Death, and Hell followed with him. And power was given unto them over the fourth part of the earth, to kill with sword, and with hunger, and with death, and with the beasts of the earth*).

With the opening of the Fourth Seal, Death himself is ushered onto the scene, riding all over the place on a horse, killing up to one-fourth of the world's remaining population. That's more than a billion people! Death will kill people with a sword. He will kill people with hunger. He will kill people with animals. He will kill people with death.

That's the bad news. The good news is, not everyone will die. In fact, three-quarters of the human race will survive! We don't know if you'll be lucky enough to be one of those, but in the event that you are (and since your odds are pretty good), let's see what kind of opportunities we can find in these new economic "conditions."

🕐 FOR NOW

ON THE ROAD AGAIN, AND AGAIN . . .

We think that with the opening of the Fourth Seal, people are going to start feeling less secure and more nervous. They'll be on the run — from the Antichrist's field operatives, from disease and drought, from Death. They're going to quit their jobs (if they still have a job), sell their homes, and start anxiously moving all over the place.

Study the graph on the next page. One line — the straight one you can barely see; that's how normal it is — illustrates what we call the "Stable Lifestyle." It shows an average family's tendency, over the course of eight weeks of normal life, to live in the same place. This is illustrated by calculating their home's distance from a fixed, stationary reference point — in this case, from a hypothetical doughnut shop called Homer's D'OHnuts.

The second, jagged line illustrates the "New Optimal Mobility for the Avoidance of Death [NOMAD] Lifestyle" and shows that family's shift, during the Tribulation, to a less stationary lifestyle. Notice how much the family moves around, altering its distance from Homer's D'OHnuts over the eight-week time frame.

As you can see, there is a big difference between the two lifestyles. The family subscribing to the Stable Lifestyle remains in the same structure over the eight-week period, so their home stays at the same distance (about thirteen miles) from the Homer's D'OHnuts reference point. The family subscribing to the NOMAD Lifestyle changes homes approximately every thirty-

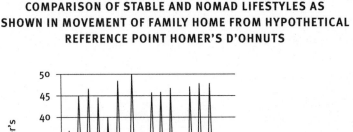

COMPARISON OF STABLE AND NOMAD LIFESTYLES AS SHOWN IN MOVEMENT OF FAMILY HOME FROM HYPOTHETICAL REFERENCE POINT HOMER'S D'OHNUTS

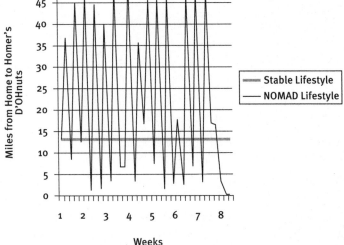

six hours, living at a broad range of distances from Homer's D'OHnuts, until finally, in the last week, actually *moving into and living in the doughnut shop itself.*

The significance of this is clear: Because more and more families will be exchanging the Stable Lifestyle for the NOMAD Lifestyle, you should invest in businesses that serve their specific needs. In fact, many aspects of American life will be turned upside down.

FAMILIAR ECONOMIC PATTERNS WILL BE DISRUPTED

Owning will be "out." Leasing will be "in." Long-term commitments to place will be "out." Short-term stays will be "in." Ownership of possessions will be "out." Rental of furnishings will be "in." Staying at home—being "in"—will be "out." Staying on the move (being "out") will be "in." Being fashionable, i.e., "in," will be "out," and being publicly gay ("out") will not matter.

Get Your Money Out Of:

* Stationary houses and stationary bicycles
* Mailbox manufacturers
* Companies that make decks, gazebos, swing sets, in-ground pools, and huge complicated barbecue grills
* Fancy furniture and appliances, interior-remodeling services, closet-remodeling services
* Home and garden centers

Put Your Money Into:

* Trailers, trailer parks, RVs, camping equipment, hovels, lean-tos, yurts
* Mailboxes R Us–type mail drops, self-storage facilities
* Trailer hitches, U-Hauls, fake front porches for mobile homes, little hibachis
* Furniture rental, appliance rental, Astroturf rental, inflatable pools
* Flowerpots, other portable "gardening" equipment

ASSAULT ON BATTERIES

When you're on the move, you're away from wall outlets. You need portable sources of energy. That's why we suggest investing in companies that manufacture or do major research in the following:

* Batteries, not only for electronics but for less obvious uses, such as dishwashers

Transient lifestyle requires alternative-energy-sourced appliances such as wind-up TV and remote, above.

+ Spring-powered wind-up devices, including children's toys, ceiling fans, and computers
+ Solar-powered appliances, including televisions, reading lamps, and blenders
+ Wind-powered devices, such as hair dryers and food processors

From Bad to Worse

Now, in one of the most significant events of the Tribulation, the Antichrist will show his true colors, which are varying shades of black, for Evil.

At the midpoint of the Tribulation, three and a half years after its start, the Antichrist will violate the seven-year covenant and turn on Israel, invading it from the north. He will abolish all forms of worship except the worship of himself and his "image." The False Prophet will create an icon (a statue, an idol, et cetera) of the Antichrist, erect it in the rebuilt Third Temple in Jerusalem, and, somehow, endow it with speech. Thus, the Antichrist will declare himself to be God. This is "the abomination that maketh desolate" (Daniel 12:11–12).

These events are set forth in Daniel 9:27 ("And he shall confirm the covenant with many for one week: and in the midst of the week he shall cause the sacrifice and the oblation to cease, and for the overspreading of abominations he shall make it desolate, even until the consummation, and that determined shall be poured upon the desolate") and Daniel 11:28–31. The "abomination of desolation" is mentioned in Matthew 24:15. The worship of the Antichrist is foretold in Revelation 13:7–8, and the revelation of the Antichrist's true nature is foreseen in 2 Thessalonians 2:3–4.

The Abomination of Desolation (or "A-bom D" or "Ab-Des" for short) is a seminal event in End Times chronology. It marks the half-way point of the Tribulation and confirms ("reveals") the ultimate evil of the Antichrist—who, you will recall, has been "indwelled" by Satan from the time of his "resurrection" about a year previous.

It's one thing for Jesus to unleash Famine and kill millions. That's business. But when the Antichrist demands to be regarded as a deity, then it's personal. God doesn't like it—and who could blame Him?

🕐 FOR NOW

WHEN YOU CARE ENOUGH TO SEND THE VERY BEAST

If the Antichrist presents himself as a god, then worship of him will be a new religion. And where there is religion, there are religious holidays. Of course we can't predict exactly what events and people he will want to commemorate, but we foresee a big market in greeting cards and gift cards for a wide range of new, evil Antichrist-centric religious holidays.

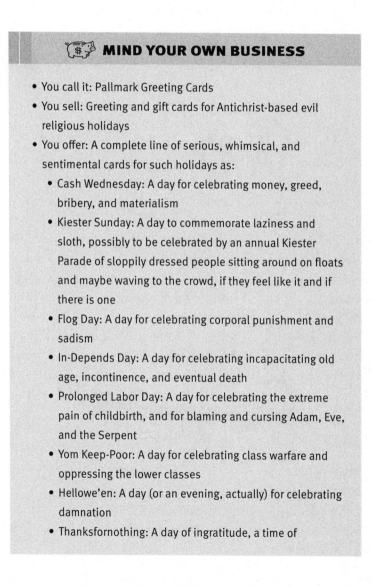

MIND YOUR OWN BUSINESS

- You call it: Pallmark Greeting Cards
- You sell: Greeting and gift cards for Antichrist-based evil religious holidays
- You offer: A complete line of serious, whimsical, and sentimental cards for such holidays as:
  - Cash Wednesday: A day for celebrating money, greed, bribery, and materialism
  - Kiester Sunday: A day to commemorate laziness and sloth, possibly to be celebrated by an annual Kiester Parade of sloppily dressed people sitting around on floats and maybe waving to the crowd, if they feel like it and if there is one
  - Flog Day: A day for celebrating corporal punishment and sadism
  - In-Depends Day: A day for celebrating incapacitating old age, incontinence, and eventual death
  - Prolonged Labor Day: A day for celebrating the extreme pain of childbirth, and for blaming and cursing Adam, Eve, and the Serpent
  - Yom Keep-Poor: A day for celebrating class warfare and oppressing the lower classes
  - Hellowe'en: A day (or an evening, actually) for celebrating damnation
  - Thanksfornothing: A day of ingratitude, a time of

selfishness, and an occasion for ignoring family and
friends
- Christmess: A day for complaining about how terrible
  Jesus was and what a blight on humanity Christianity has
  been

Happy Thanksfornothing card celebrates Antichrist's ingratitude and
lack of appreciation for life's blessings

FOR LATER

WHOLE LOTTA SHAKIN' GOIN' TO GO ON

Now is the time — before the Fifth Seal is opened and, worse, the Sixth — to clean up your portfolio and prepare for new trends.

We want you to *buy* stock in:

* The company that makes Astroturf, and any other companies you can find that make artificial turf
* Fish hatcheries and other man-made sources of seafood
* Companies that make "krab" or "crabbe" or "qrabb" or "krabbe" or "k-rab" or any other artificial crablike seafood or "seafoode" or whatever

We want you to *sell* stock in:

* Any logging, paper, lumber, timber, or other companies dealing with trees or wood
* Any shipping companies, by which we mean companies that literally use ships that move across oceans or lakes (transcontinental shippers that use rail or air are okay, at least for now)

And we want you to sell or stay away from any companies that have anything to do with mountains and/or islands. Can you guess why?

a. The skiing and summer resort industries are going to take a beating.
b. We just happen not to like mountains or islands.
c. The mountains and islands of the world are soon going to start moving around.

✒ FEARFULLY ASKED QUESTIONS (FAQ) ✒

Q. If everyone dies from Death, is the Tribulation over?

A. It would be if they did, but they don't. Only about a quarter of the human race dies. That leaves three out of every four people still alive. If you know four people, three will still be alive. Even if you only know two people, odds are that you'll make it. Of course, if you know only one person, he'll die, and you won't know anyone else. And if you know only three people, the one who ends up dying could be you. Look, just go out and meet at least three people and you'll be able to survive the Fourth Seal and get ready for the Fifth (Martyrs of the Tribulation Cry Out to the Lord).

Q. I'm not sure I understand the Abomination of Desolation. Can you explain it?

A. An abomination is a very bad thing. Desolation is a feeling of deep sadness. So the term "the Abomination of Desolation" can be translated as "the Bad Thing That Makes You Sad."

Q. Why does the Antichrist, who by now is indwelled by Satan himself, want to be called God? Is he having an identity crisis?

A. Actually, it's Satan who is having the identity crisis. In fact, his whole life has been one big identity crisis, from the time he was an angel and rebelled against God. Now he's transferred that crisis to the Antichrist. This seems rather unfair, yes, but remember: He's Satan. He's not "about" being fair.

CHAPTER 9

Tribulation Midpoint

We're halfway through! Things are going to get even more tumultuous, so let's pause, catch our breath, and review everything that's happened over the past three and a half years:

+ More than 1.4 billion Christians have spontaneously levitated, naked, to Heaven, leaving behind their unmanned cars and planes, prostheses, pets, and many relatives (including children) who didn't believe in Jesus quite enough.
+ One man has united the world.
+ He's made a seven-year covenant with Israel.
+ More than a billion not-Christian-enough Christians and Muslims the world over have allowed the Jews to rebuild the Third Temple on the Dome of the Rock / Temple Mount in Jerusalem. It is once again the site of animal sacrifice and the center of Judaism.
+ The world leader (who is, in fact, the Antichrist) has required everyone to wear his special number (666) on their foreheads or right hands. Those who haven't have been captured and executed.
+ The Antichrist has been killed and has come back to life.
+ After losing a war in Heaven with the Archangel Michael, Satan has been cast down to Earth, where he has "indwelled" the Antichrist and endowed him with satanic powers.

✦ Elijah and, probably, Moses have reappeared after an absence of five thousand years and are walking around Jerusalem, promoting Jesus by, among other things, issuing fire out of their mouths.

✦ War (possibly nuclear, but more likely with bucklers and shields), plus Famine, plus "Death," have killed a total of one-quarter of the world's post-Rapture population, or about 1.28 billion people.

✦ The Antichrist has violated his covenant and turned against Israel. His chief promoter (the False Prophet) has placed an image of the Antichrist in the Third Temple and endowed it with speech, proclaiming it a god. That—as opposed to the billion people killed—is the "abomination that maketh desolate."

In light of all this, make sure that you:

☛ have properly incorporated your small business(es) as an LLP, S-Corp, et cetera with state and federal tax authorities. If in doubt about which form of incorporation is right for you, consult an attorney. He or she should be qualified to advise on corporate tax matters, and still be alive;

☛ have reviewed your credit rating and informed the major credit-rating services (Experian, Trans-Union, Equifax) that you will report them to the Antichrist if they fail to correct any inaccuracies;

☛ know—or, actually, make sure everyone else knows—the location of your will (remember our tip: Mount it with magnets on your fridge), power-of-attorney, and emergency sardines.

CHAPTER 10

Persecution of the Christians (and Jews, Too)

Witness of the Persecution

Some people, for whatever reason, won't worship the Antichrist. These will include Christians who stay true to Christ and Jews who refuse the Antichrist's Mark®. He will persecute them all over the world, as was foreseen in 2 Thessalonians 2:4 and Revelation 13:4–8.

🕐 FOR NOW

Call us old-fashioned, but as Jews we have a real issue with persecution. So we're not entirely comfortable with the idea of cashing in on it. As we have shown, there are plenty of ways to make money during the Tribulation without having to exploit the deliberate oppression of one group of people by another.

But that's us. You may feel, as many do about investing in various unpleasant or unfortunate areas of life, that "it isn't personal. It's business." If so, here's an idea about how to make money in the coming bull market in persecution.

SOFTWARE FOR HARD TIMES

All the Christians who have, since the Rapture, accepted and stayed true to Jesus, and all the Jews who refuse allegiance to the Antichrist: That's a lot of people to persecute! How will the persecutors (the Antichrist and his "people"—assuming they are people and not demons) keep track of them all? How will they coordinate their activities? How will they avoid wasting time and resources persecuting people who have already *been* persecuted?

By using software that you (or people you hire) develop.

🐷 MIND YOUR OWN BUSINESS

- You call it: Perfect Persecutor
- You sell: A persecution-management program to keep track of who-oppressed-or-killed-whom, with what, where, and when
- You offer: Public-sector management solutions to help governments improve efficiency and accountability through next-generation database, middleware, and applications development, usage, and troubleshooting

Look, we know you don't know beans about writing software. So just find some computer science majors and pay them minimum wage plus whatever the End Times, famine-ravaged-society equivalent is of Red Bull and pizza. They'll be thrilled to have a job, not to mention something to eat.

And once you've made your first sale to the Antichrist and his persecution unit, stand by. Sooner or later, Microsoft will offer to buy you out and fold the program into Windows. When that happens, just take the money and run. Within a year, any twelve year old with a laptop and broadband will be able to oversee his own global persecution network. The sector will be "over."

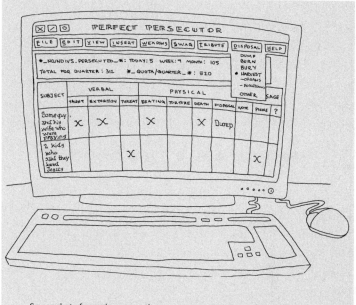

Screenshot of sample persecution-management program. Supports "Drag 'n' Drop" for tallying dead bodies user has dragged and/or dropped.

FOR LATER ⏱

HEDGING YOUR BET, BETTING YOUR HEDGE

We want you to start looking into hedge funds.

No, not those complicated and esoteric "funds-of-funds" that you need a zillion dollars to get into, that cost an arm and a leg in fees and commissions, and that are not only beyond the comprehension of our readers but of us, too.

Instead, we want you to look into funds that *literally invest in hedges*—plus shrubs, sod, ground cover, and other horticultural services such as nurseries and landscaping.

Can you guess why?

a. Jesus will be coming back soon, and we want the environment to look nice for Him.

b. We have started our own Hedge, Sod, and Ground Ivy Fund, and hope to trick you into investing in it.

c. All hell is going to break loose with nature, and there will be a big spike in demand for plants, landscaping, and so forth.

🖋 FEARFULLY ASKED QUESTIONS (FAQ) 🖋

Q. If my software company gets going, wouldn't it be better to do an IPO than to wait around for Microsoft to offer to buy me out?

A. Normally, yes. But these are the End Times. Three and a half years into the Tribulation, venture capitalists and private investors will all be broke and living in bombed-out warehouses in Palo Alto. The only computer company still pursuing business as usual will be Microsoft, still working out the bugs in Vista.

Q. How can I get in on the ground floor of the exciting new field of professional persecution?

A. Stay in school! Unless school is destroyed in an earthquake. In that case, look for courses you can take online. And don't forget to ask if you can receive course credit for any real-life experience you've had harassing, tormenting, bullying, and beating up people during the years prior to enrollment. You may be required to produce affidavits from persons you persecuted affirming that you did indeed bully them and beat them up. Ask them nicely to sign a document that you (or the school's admissions department) draw up. If they express a disinclination to sign or even to be in the same room with you, threaten to beat them up again.

CHAPTER 11

The Fifth Seal

Martyrs of the Tribulation Cry Out to the Lord

A Reasonable Request

The next seal triggers an event that takes place in Heaven. So it probably won't affect our financial decisions down here on Earth very much. But it has a whole seal to itself, so it's worth noting.

> In Heaven, with the opening of the Fifth Seal, the Christians who were martyred during the first half of the Tribulation beg God to avenge their deaths. They are told to wait until others are killed and join them. All this is predicted in 2 Timothy 3:12 and in Revelation 6:9–11.

The "Tribulation martyrs" will be people who, although they "didn't make the first cut" in the Rapture, come to Christ during the first three and a half years of the Tribulation and are killed for their faith.

🕐 FOR NOW

There's nothing to do for now. Even we can't think of ways to make money on stuff that takes place in Heaven.

FOR LATER 🧭

ABROAD AT HOME

Soon—with the opening of the Sixth Seal, in the next chapter—a number of terrible geological cataclysms are going to shake the Earth.

And that's bad news for vacationers, honeymooners, and globe-trotters. What do you say to someone who has her heart set on a week in Venice (Italy), when the city no longer exists? How do you console a couple who have planned for years on a trip to Paris (France), when the City of Lights has become a Cauldron of Hellish Decimation?

You provide a replacement destination. And you make a nice small business out of it.

🐷 MIND YOUR OWN BUSINESS

- You call it: Substitourism "International"
- You sell: Travel to locations all over the United States with names *exactly identical* to those of the world's most famous and beloved tourist destinations
- You offer: Attractive getaways and travel deals to places not devastated, torn by riots and looting, or under water. These are destinations for which American travelers won't need a passport, will already know the language, and will already hold and understand the currency.

Just look at this partial list of possible Substitourist "International" destinations:

Venice, California	Egypt, Vermont
Paris, Texas	Egypt, Maine

Jamaica, Queens

Nassau, Long Island

Rome, New York

Athens, New York

Athens, Georgia

Egypt, Pennsylvania

Egypt, Alabama

Italy, South Carolina

Moscow, Idaho

England, Oklahoma

Russia, Ohio

Germany, Georgia

China, Indiana

Brazil, Kentucky

We're sure there are others, but these should be enough to get you started. And can we suggest a possible slogan? "Let's (Kinda, Sorta) Go!"

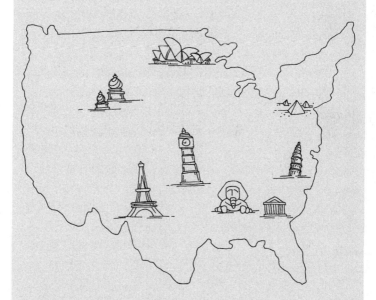

Some popular Substitourism landmarks—proving that "There's no place like home."

HOME, RELATIVELY SWEET HOME

Think about buying stock in anything having to do with the home: home improvement, furnishings, home entertainment, et cetera, assuming some homes are still left. Why?

a. Because, for reasons to be explained later, suddenly everyone on Earth will decide to get married and "settle down."
b. Because home-decoration magazines will coerce everyone into making "nesting" come back big.
c. Because once the Sixth Seal is opened, no one will want to go outside.

⚡ FEARFULLY ASKED QUESTIONS (FAQ) ⚡

Q. How can we be sure there will be any Parises left standing anywhere as a substitourist destination? What if both Paris, France, *and* Paris, Texas, are destroyed?

A. Relax. There are forty-three towns named Paris in the United States alone. There are three each in Arkansas, Illinois, Kentucky, and Ohio. That's a dozen Parises, with thirty-one more left over (source: http://www.placesnamed.com/p/a/paris.asp). One of them has to make it through.

Q. We're planning a trip to Paris, Mississippi. Should we hate the people we see there, the way we would normally hate the French if we went to Paris, France?

A. Why not? It might enhance your trip. And if "hate" seems too much, at least feel free to find the natives of Paris, Mississippi, to be snooty, rude, and haughty, and to be appalled that they smoke too much.

CHAPTER 12

The Sixth Seal

Signs in the Sky

More Bad News

With the opening of the Sixth Seal, things go from worse to even more worse. Of course you could say that at any point during the Tribulation, but just look:

> The opening of the Sixth Seal will set off a series of terrible geological and celestial phenomena, as foretold in Revelation 6:12–14. This was also predicted in Matthew 24:29 and Joel 2:30–31.

Here is what will happen when Jesus opens the Sixth Seal:

1. *There will be a huge earthquake.* We don't know where it will be centered or whether it will trigger tsunamis.

2. *The sun will become black.* Forever? Or just for a while? Will it still give off heat? Will day turn to night? And if so, what will night turn to?

3. *The stars will fall onto the Earth.* At first we thought "stars" was a metaphor for what would actually be meteorites, which didn't seem so bad. Then we realized that we don't know how

big they'll be or how many will fall or where they'll land, or if they'll maybe be real stars, and we decided that in fact it would be very, very bad after all.

4. *The heaven will "depart as a scroll when it is rolled away."* We admit we find this slightly confusing. Is "the heaven" actually the sky? How can the sky "roll away"? What's behind it? Outer space? What we call the sky is, of course, the atmosphere. Does that mean Earth's atmosphere will "roll away"? That would be terrible.

5. *"Every mountain and island" will be moved "out of their places."* Horrifying *and* (uncharacteristically, for Revelation) ungrammatical. (Shouldn't every mountain and island be moved out of *its* place?) Plus, we don't like that "every." It's one thing for little islands like St. John's or Maui or even Tasmania to move around. Remember, though, that the entire continent-nation of Australia is actually an island! And so are Japan, and Manhattan, and England! This will be absolutely horrible unless they move just a few inches. And what about the mountains? The Rockies, the Appalachians, the Alps, the Pyrenees, the Urals, the Andes, the Himalayas—the whole thing is very distressing.

6. *The moon will become "as blood."* We assume that "as blood" means that the moon will just turn red, and not literally be transformed into a liquid, which would be absurd—and also wet, which is just disgusting.

In the previous chapter we told you to invest in anything having to do with the home—furnishings, decoration, home-improvement centers, et cetera. Now you know why. With these hideous ongoing calamities, most people aren't going to want to go outside—especially those who live anywhere near where the islands and the mountains will be moving around. And, by the way, Scripture doesn't tell us if any of them will ever *stop* moving.

Of course, if an island or a mountain is heading right for your house, you will indeed go outside and run for your life. Otherwise, though, you'll probably remain indoors like everybody else—and, like everybody else, you'll start to look for ways to make your home more comfortable and attractive, not to mention increase its resale value. Once those "stars" start falling to the Earth, look for home-improvement stocks to take off!

🕐 FOR NOW

STAY IN WITH THE IN CROWD

Just because people will be terrified to go outside doesn't mean their normal needs will disappear. They'll still require the services of doctors, dentists, addiction therapy groups, fitness coaches, marriage counselors, and hairstylists. They'll still want their kids to take piano or judo or dance lessons. They'll still want their relationships with whoever's left—their parents, their golf buddies, their adulterous lovers, et cetera—to be maintained.

But how can you make use of those services, or keep up those relationships, if you never leave the house?

You can if you know about My-Guys™, which we recommend as a possible addition to your long-term portfolio. My-Guys not only brings everything and everyone *to you*, from dog walkers to psycho-pharmacologists, but they do what you would do if only you could leave the house. *They* visit your mother. *They* sneak out to a tryst with your lover to keep your affair going. *They* do *your* jogging, Pilates, or yoga. They detail your car, to be sure it's sparkling clean inside and out, in case you ever get a chance to use it again — and then they drive it to your AA meeting and speak *for you* (and using your first name).

Who are these "guys"? Some are ex-military — Green Berets, Navy SEALS, Delta Force, "black ops," Special Forces, Special Ops, Delta-Ones, "wet ops," Wet Ones, Rangers, Marine FAST. They like to live dangerously and don't mind getting paid to do so. Others are ex–private contractors (Blackwater, Triple Canopy, et cetera), which means they're ex-ex-military.

With their armor-plated Hummers, their lethal martial arts skills, and their (perfectly legal, registered) assault weapons, they take your kids to piano lessons, soccer games, and birthday parties. Or, if you don't want your kids to go outside, My-Guys 4 Kidz will go in your children's place and take their music, ballet, or karate lessons for them. Feel like a leisurely stroll down Main Street but just too terrified to try? My-Guys do it for you, stopping to gaze longingly at the items in whatever unbroken shop windows remain — the very items that you would gaze at, if only you could. For a small additional fee, My-Guys will make an audio or video recording of the experience as a permanent keepsake of their/your experience.

They do it all. You don't do any of it. You and your loved ones stay inside, safe and secure. And, because My-Guys hires hundreds of ophthalmologists and golf foursomes and middle-aged-women-in-sweat-suits-doing-tai-chi-in-the-park at a time, they take advantage of economies of scale — and pass the savings along to you.

Jews *Really* for Jesus

If you happen to have 144,000 virgin Jewish men as Facebook friends, you may get a phone call around now.

> Although it is unclear exactly when this will happen, 144,000
> Jewish evangelists will roam the Earth, proselytizing for Christ.
> Each of the twelve tribes of Israel will be represented by 12,000
> men, all of whom will have some sort of seal from God on their
> foreheads.

This event is highly controversial in biblical circles. Some say the 144,000 are "the Church," although many sources, including Tim LaHaye, in *Revelation Unveiled,* insist they are Jews. There is also disagreement over whether they are virgins. Those who believe it point to Revelation 14:3–4, which tells of 144,000 men gathered (later) in Heaven. Verse 4 says, *"These are they which were not defiled with women; for they are virgins. These are they which follow the Lamb whithersoever he goeth. These were redeemed from among men, being the firstfruits unto God and to the Lamb."*

Frankly, we're somewhat put off by that "defiled with women" part. Then again, this was written by a hermit in a cave on a tiny Greek island between AD 68 and 96. Maybe he just didn't know any nondefiling women.

🕐 FOR NOW

THY BEAUTIFUL LAUNDRETTE
If we know nothing else about 144,000 wandering, proselytizing virgins — Jewish or not — we know two things: They have money (since they certainly don't spend it on rent, mortgages, families, dates, or nightlife), and they dress in pure, undefiled white.

Put those two facts together, and it equals a potentially exciting new way for you to "clean up":

🐷 MIND YOUR OWN BUSINESS

- You call it: White Here, White Now
- You sell: On-site traveling laundry services to the 144,000
- You offer: Robe, garment, and raiment washing, bleaching, ironing, and folding, plus spot fabric repair, custom alterations, et cetera

Of course, it's not as if all 144,000 of "the boys" will be traveling in a group. (Although if a mob of that size "suggested" that we accept Jesus, we'd think very seriously before saying no.) On the contrary, we think they'll be traveling in pairs all throughout the world. So ask around and find out where groups of them congregate on their off-hours, and set up shop there.

And be sure to charge premium prices. They can afford it.

Part IV The Tribulation: The Trumpet Judgments

CHAPTER 13

The Day of the Lord, and the Seventh Seal

We're about to introduce the next series of horrific disasters, known as the Trumpet Judgments, after which will come the Bowl Judgments. Taken together, these two sequences of catastrophe are known as the Day of the Lord.

They're the final two stages of the Tribulation before the actual Second Coming of Jesus Christ. (His appearance in the clouds to greet the Raptured doesn't count as a "coming.") That means we have maybe two years—three, tops—to keep making money.

So get ready for some unusual financial strategies. The Trumpet Judgments are going to bring to an end not only a third of the remaining human race, but also many of the familiar ways of earning wealth (working for a salary, owning a business, offering professional services, et cetera). So we're going to show you some creative ways to attain financial success even while the world, society, and the Earth itself are collapsing all around you.

Part of this strategy will involve selling whatever stocks and bonds you may still be holding. Global cataclysms are coming, and they're going to hurt. Various industries will change in stark, rapid, and profound (and, believe us, negative) ways. That's why, in the next part of this book, we've put our "sell" advice under the urgent headline "Dump and Jump." When we tell you to sell this or that sector of securities, we mean it. *Get the hell out, pronto.*

The Trumpet Judgments are going to be "interesting," and if you're still around when they're over and the Bowl Judgments begin you'll be ready to enjoy a well-earned retirement, however briefly. We'll give you tips on how to make use of your time as well as instructions on how to protect your retirement resources until the very last second leading up to the Battle of Armageddon.

A Really Hot Opening Act

According to Revelation 8:1, when the Seventh Seal is opened, there will be silence in Heaven for about half an hour. (The normal sounds of Heaven are those of joy and praise for God. That, by the way, is how we know Heaven isn't in outer space. There is no air in space. In space, not only can no one hear you scream, they can't hear you singing songs of adoration, either.) Then seven angels will receive trumpets, which they will blow one by one, unleashing a series of terrible judgments on mankind.

First, however, there will be a kind of warm-up event as an angel throws fire at us.

> After the heavenly silence, an angel will burn incense and hurl fire at the Earth. We learn this from Revelation 8:3–5 (3: And another angel came and stood at the altar, having a golden censer; and there was given unto him much incense. . . . 5: And the angel took the censer, and filled it with fire of the altar, and cast it into the earth: and there were voices, and thunderings, and lightnings, and an earthquake).

Thunderings and lightnings and an earthquake are nothing new, but those "voices" are telling us three things:

1. The First Trumpet is about to be blown.
2. From now on, make sure any life, home ownership, or prop-

erty insurance you buy has *no* clause exempting claims based on force majeure. Once the trumpets get started, life on planet Earth is going to be all force all majeure all the time.

3. *Get rid of any investments you have in trees and grass.* In other words . . .

Dump and Jump

Sell any investments you have in golf courses, timber, lumber, building materials, and all wood- or tree-based manufacturing, such as furniture, paper, chopsticks, Japanese lanterns, and toothpicks. Also sod farms, Christmas tree farms, and lawn and garden centers. Lawn mowers, seeders, hedgers, string trimmers, lawn fertilizer—just everything connected with grass, period.

CHAPTER 14

The First Trumpet

Hail and Fire

> Finally, the first angel will blow the First Trumpet. This will cause
> hail and fire to fall to Earth and bring about the destruction of a
> third of the planet's trees and all of the grass. This is duly fore-
> told in Revelation 8:7 (*7: The first angel sounded, and there fol-
> lowed hail and fire mingled with blood, and they were cast upon
> the earth: and the third part of trees was burnt up, and all green
> grass was burnt up*).

Now you see why we said to get out of grass: It's all gone, as
are one-third of the trees. If you took our advice, you're sigh-
ing with relief, although it may be mingled with abject terror.
If you didn't listen, and held on to your timber, toothpick, and
chopstick stocks, well . . . Get rid of them now. And learn to pay
attention to our next Dump and Jump.

We didn't suggest selling your holdings in sports teams because
baseball can be played on Astroturf, and the teams can switch to
metal bats if they have to. Football can be played on " 'Turf," too,
and basketball teams play indoors. In fact, because most fans will
choose to stay at home, all *televised* sports will thrive—except
for golf, for reasons explained later, and NASCAR, because most
of its owners, drivers, and pit crews will be in Heaven.

The More Things Change, the More They'll Become Different

Here are some of the financial and retail trends we predict for the period of the Trumpet Judgments:

1. The Shrinking of the Market: Over a quarter of the Earth's original population will have been killed by now, and many more will die as our Heavenly Father's marvelous plan for us continues to unfold. This translates into fewer customers available to buy goods and services.

And that raises a troubling concern: How can a seller make a profit in an ever-dwindling "universe" of buyers?

Fortunately, American ingenuity solved this problem a long time ago. You increase your profits as a seller by *turning your buyers into sellers,* who then pass some of their profits back to you! It's called multilevel marketing (or network marketing). Often abbreviated as MLM, it is the genius behind such companies as Amway and Herbalife.

It works like this: You sell product P to buyer B. Then you offer buyer B the opportunity to become a "distributor" of product P and sell it to others. B buys from you (or the company) the stock, materials, brochures, et cetera necessary to sell more product, and passes along to you part of his or her profits from those sales.

This can go on for several generations or more, with "sponsor" sellers at the top of the line making profits from their "downline," and those below creating downlines of their own. You, as the originating sponsor of this expanding pyramid of salespeople, can earn income from three, four, or even more generations. Your potential profits are limited only by the number of people actually buying anything from the downest downline, or the number of people in your sales team who quit or, in this particular period in history, die.

We look for MLM to undergo a vigorous expansion during the Trumpet Judgments, especially in the distribution and sales of these essential goods:

- ✔ food
- ✔ alcoholic beverages
- ✔ human organs
- ✔ military-grade weapons
- ✔ legal and illicit pharmaceuticals
- ✔ functional MP3 players
- ✔ healthy babies
- ✔ gasoline
- ✔ potable water
- ✔ toilet paper
- ✔ antibiotics
- ✔ pornography

Pick one (or more) of these products and form a network of "sales associates." Then sit back and watch as you start reaping the rewards of a healthy downline, while all you do is relax at home, fend off intruders, and keep away from the windows.

2. The Losing-of-Its-Mind of the Economy: It would seem that as more and more people die while the world's money supply remains stable, everyone would get richer. After all, you would think that if the "pie" stays the same "size" after most people in the "diner" are "killed" by "a short-order cook" who goes "nuts" because he is "indwelled by Satan," then whoever is left alive will get that much larger a "slice" than they otherwise would. And you would be right!

However, as with most things in life, good news at one end of the equation is balanced by bad news at the other. Just as inflation occurs when "too much money chases too few goods," once enough people die we will experience a kind of inverse inflation, in which too much money will be in the hands of too few consumers. The result will be grim—not enough people spending too much money chasing not enough commodities too fast in not enough time over too much space, creating "just-in-time" surpluses too late to be enough and too early to be just-in-time.

It's a disturbing scenario, but we have some ideas to help you cope with it.

3. The Death of List Price

> Q. Why did G-d create goyim?
> A. *Somebody* has to buy retail.
> — OLD JEWISH JOKE

The Jewish people have an extensive mercantile history. In the beginning, the pursuit of trade came naturally to them, as it does to all nomadic peoples. Later, in the Middle Ages, their exclusion from the guilds left urban Jews few alternatives for earning a living. Since then, the role of middleman, of the peddler who buys something wholesale from X and then sells it retail to Y, has been traditionally associated with Jews.

But such an arrangement can only exist if there are more customers than middlemen—as has been the case from the earliest days of capitalism.

This state of affairs will begin to crumble as the Trumpet Judgments proceed, for a paradoxical reason. During the Tribulation, Jews will fulfill a special role. As God's originally Chosen People—the first people to acknowledge that God *was* God, and the people among whom Jesus was born—the Jews will be spared God's wrath. (They haven't been spared the Antichrist's wrath, but let's face it: You can't be spared everything.)

That's great news for Jews (at least for a while), but it will have a distorting effect on the world economy. As the Trumpet Judgments unfold, the number of Jews in the world will remain relatively stable, while the number of Gentiles will sharply decline. Jews, in other words, will form a larger and larger percentage of the world population.

This will lead to a staggering result: We will face a world in which *almost no one will be left to buy retail.* In outright defiance of the laws of economics, almost everyone will be buying wholesale. The world economy will be like a rock band consisting entirely of lead singers, or a football team completely composed of quarterbacks. The long-term (i.e., five-month) effects of this will include declining profits, increased corporate centralization, unstable employment rates, wild currency fluctuations, and the entire global economy grinding to a halt on Rosh Hashanah and Yom Kippur.

And, as if that weren't bad enough, there's this:

Dump and Jump

Sell anything and everything connected with the **shipping, seafood,** or **vacation resort industries** of **Egypt, Israel, Lebanon, Syria, Turkey, Greece, Albania, Montenegro, Bosnia and Herzegovina, Croatia, Slovenia, Italy, Monaco, France, Spain, Corsica, Sardinia, Morocco, Algeria, Tunisia,** and **Libya.**

CHAPTER 15

The Second Trumpet

A Meteor

At the Second Trumpet, *"as it were a great mountain burning with fire"* will be *"cast into the sea."* When it hits, it will turn one-third of the sea into blood, kill one-third of the sea's marine life, and destroy one-third of the ships afloat. This is predicted in Revelation 8:8–9.

Some experts say this mountain-like object will actually be an asteroid or meteorite, ablaze from its descent through the atmosphere. As for the "sea" it lands in, opinion is split. Is the reference simply to the Mediterranean? Or to "the sea" in general, which would include the planet's oceans?

Similarly, the wording "a third part of the ships" could mean one of two things: either one-third of the total number of ships in "the sea" will be completely destroyed, or one-third of the structure of each individual ship will be destroyed — either in the Mediterranean alone or on all the seas.

We frankly can't decide which is the intended prophecy (neither can the experts, as usual), so we're going to split the difference. We're going to calculate the change in world population based on the assumption that this "mountain" will affect all the Earth's seas and oceans and all its seagoing vessels.

Which means that the effects wrought by the Second Trumpet are going to be grim *apart* from the killing of one-third of all marine life and the turning-to-blood of one-third of the seas and oceans.

We estimate that at any given time, there are approximately 30.782 million people at sea around the world. We derived this figure from Web sites featuring statistics concerning the world's principle navies, the fishing industry, the shipping industry, the pleasure boat industry, and the pleasure cruise industry. Therefore, when one-third of the ships are destroyed, we interpret that to mean that one-third of this total are killed.

That number comes to 10.26 million people.

In terms of investments, however, we're going to focus on the Mediterranean. That's why we told you to Dump and Jump out of all sea-based industries set in and around that body of water.

Go with the Flow

There is one form of investment that we think will become increasingly popular during this period. Commonly referred to as "investing in cash flow," these investments are technically termed *viaticals*.

When you invest in a viatical, you buy a payout entitlement from its holder at a steep discount on the amount due. The holder walks away with a lump sum that is less than he would have received over time but is in his hands today. You then hold the note for its complete term and receive the full amount due.

For example, say someone wins a lottery and decides on the annuity-type payout of $1 million per year for twenty years. Then, a year later, that person decides, for whatever reason, that he wants a lump sum after all. He sells the rights to the payout to you for, say, $5 million. *You* now receive the payout. In five years, you recoup your investment. Everything you receive starting in year six and thereafter is profit. The same principle applies to life insurance benefits, lawsuit awards, and pension obligations, assuming they are transferable.

These kinds of investments are controversial because in many cases the seller can do much better simply by keeping the obligation, taking out a loan for the lump sum he wants today (perhaps using the note as collateral), and paying it off over time.

But, what with mountains falling into seas and all the grass in the world burning up, many people will panic and decide that there *is* no time. They'll be glad to sell you their lottery tickets or lawsuit awards, often for such relatively modest considerations as a case of sardines in mustard sauce or an uncontaminated box of Band-Aids.

Sweet, yes — but then what? You know even more specifically than they do that Jesus will arrive in less than two years, at which point all bets (and all viaticals) will be off. How, then, can you make a profit on the note for which you've just paid a perfectly good case of canned fish?

Get this.

MIND YOUR OWN BUSINESS

- You call it: Viatical Sabbatical, Inc.
- You sell: The viaticals you buy from people, *back to the original issuers*
- You offer: Relief from crushing obligations, to debt-burdened lottery commissions, defendants, and pension funds

Contact the state or regional lottery commission or the defendant in the lawsuit or the insurance company, and offer to "settle" for 50 or even 25 percent. They'll leap at the chance to retire the obligation at a discount, you'll walk away with a tidy profit, and no one except you will know that they could have hung on until the Second Coming and gotten away much more cheaply.

Or, take advantage of the general confusion and make a killing in the following unorthodox kinds of viaticals.

🐷 MIND YOUR OWN BUSINESS

- You call it: Radical Viaticals!
- You sell: Peace of mind and cash in hand. Security today, not some time in the unpredictable future.
- You offer: To buy these "payout obligations" at a discount:

1. Kids' allowances: Children can be notoriously impatient and are thus easily persuaded to accept pennies on the dollar for their future allowance receivables. Have an attorney draw up some legal-sounding document requiring the kids' parents to pay you in accordance with the kids' instructions.

2. Huge garbage bags of aluminum soda cans: Half viatical investment, half commodities trading, still: Each can represents an obligation by the state to pay the bearer on demand. Only applies to states that redeem cans, obviously.

3. Frequent-flier miles: During the End Times, many people who have accumulated significant numbers of frequent-flier miles will be too distraught, ill, or terrified to use them. You should be able to buy them up cheap and realize their value in two ways.

- First, research which flights are most often overbooked. Convert your miles into a ticket on one of those flights. Go to the airport, get through security, and go to the gate. When the flight is announced as being overbooked, agree to accept the airline's cash compensation in return for taking a later flight (to a place to which you have no intention of going).
- Then, sell the ticket (for the later flight) for cash at what will surely become a bustling black market in secondhand,

counterfeit, and stolen airline tickets at every major airport. Such bazaars wil probably gather at each terminal's baggage claim area, where periodic chaos is the norm. If you can't sell directly to an actual passenger, sell to a middleman and get out.

Giving a child a few dollars in exchange for his allowance from now until the Second Coming can be a useful addition to your portfolio—and a great way to get ahead.

And remember to—

Dump and Jump

*Get out of stocks in companies dealing with **instant anything** (beverages, fiber supplements, et cetera), as well as companies dealing with **white-water rafting, freshwater fish,** and **river-based leisure activities.** In fact, just bail out of everything that requires **fresh-** or **tap water.** Now.*

CHAPTER 16

The Third Trumpet

Wormwood Falls from the Heavens

> This somewhat puzzling (but still horrible) judgment will take place when the third angel sounds the Third Trumpet: A "great star" will fall on "a third of the rivers" and make them bitter, killing all who depend on them for water. This is foretold in Revelation 8:10–11 (*10: And the third angel sounded, and there fell a great star from heaven, burning as it were a lamp, and it fell upon the third part of the rivers, and upon the fountains of waters; 11: And the name of the star is called Wormwood: and the third part of the waters became wormwood; and many men died of the waters, because they were made bitter*).

Tim LaHaye explains that this "great star" is a meteorite, which hits "at just the right spot" and so "pollutes the water supply of a third of the earth's rivers." He notes, "Evidently there is a place in the earth where the headwaters of three great rivers come together."

As for wormwood, it's (we looked it up) a bitter herb used for centuries as an insect repellent. It was also used to make absinthe, and one of its species is tarragon. Apparently there is a star in the heavens called Wormwood, which is also *made* of wormwood. If it fell to the Earth, it would certainly catch fire and burn like a lamp (or "torch," in some translations) as it plunged through the atmosphere (unless that had actually been rolled back at the opening of the Sixth Seal, earlier). Such a flaming mass of herb, coming into contact with a confluence of headwaters, would create a gigantic infusion—a sort of titanic cauldron of wormwood "tea"—that would indeed make the river waters extremely bitter.

So we urge you to get out of companies whose products have to be mixed with potable water. When that "star" lands and pollutes the rivers, water is going to take a hit. No one is going to want to mix their Crystal Light or Metamucil or Tang with horrible wormwood tea, no matter how fat, irregular, or thirsty they are.

Back to the Futures

The pollution of much of the Earth's lakes and rivers will have many consequences, from the decline and fall of the Starbucks empire to the destruction of the water pistol industry. But, as always, we want to focus on the good news. Where, in this catastrophe of unparalleled magnitude, is the money?

We've come up with a new kind of investment vehicle with which to exploit this exciting albeit tragic event. It's based on the premise that canned and bottled goods produced before the Third Trumpet Judgment will soar in value once freshwater the world over is contaminated.

💲 MIND YOUR OWN BUSINESS

- You call it: The (*Your Name Here*) Micro-Futures Exchange
- You sell: Shares in a scarce commodity
- You offer: A primary market in valuable food, and a secondary market for speculators and investors

To start your own Micro-Futures Exchange, simply do the following:

1. Get hold of a good-sized can or bottle of some food product in which water is a key ingredient — in other words, anything, as long as it doesn't require refrigeration. Canned vegetables, tuna packed in water, Perrier, and pickles are great. So are bottled juices, canned soups, and even still water itself, as long as it was bottled before the Wormwood star landed.

2. Announce, via computer bulletin boards and chat groups, or just by nailing signs to trees, that you are selling "shares" in the contents of the can or bottle. Specify the number of shares and the price per share. Also announce that you will open the can or bottle on a certain date and time in the future. (Refer to that as the "call date" or "strike date" or some other financial-sounding name.) At that time you will split the contents with the shareholders pro rata, depending on who holds how many shares.

3. Make sure your customers know that they can trade their shares in a "commodity futures" market that you run. But remind everyone that, as with all investments, there is an element of risk: What if the contents of the can or bottle have spoiled? What if other cans or bottles of the same product appear on the market before the call date arrives, lessening the value of yours? And, of course, there is also the possibility of gain: What if further disasters make the contents even more valuable?

4. Supervise the trading of the shares and charge a fee for each transaction.

5. At the appointed time, open the can or bottle and distribute the contents accordingly.

We call this "monetizing scarcity." You'll call it "cashing in big on the packing fluids in a can of garbanzo beans." Whatever it's called, we like how it rewards risk and entrepreneurial zeal (you bought the can first), aids in the distribution of essential goods (shareholders all get a portion of the cranberry-apple drink or whatever), and, of course, puts money in your pocket. It's a win-win-win!

So celebrate once you've completed the transaction. But don't forget to do this next:

Dump and Jump

Liquidate any holdings in companies that have anything to do with the outside: construction, some sports, agriculture, shipping. Anything that deals with oceans or lakes. All transportation, including automobiles, boats, planes, and trucks, and their respective parts providers and fuel refiners, distributors, and sellers. Also amusement parks and outdoor apparel. Don't forget to pull out of sunblock, helicopters, Rollerblades, Segways, and aerospace. Bail on camping and recreation, bicycles, mass transit, and gardening. Sell immediately snowboards. Billboards. Surfboards. Boogie boards, diving boards — just every kind of board except bulletin boards and emery boards. In fact, the hell with it — just sell everything. Any stock, bond, REIT, mutual fund, T-bill, derivative, option, future, savings bond, and every other investment instrument you may still be holding on to, regardless of its sector or field. Outside — which is, let's face it, where everything ultimately comes from — is "over."

CHAPTER 17

The Fourth Trumpet
The Darkening of a Third of the Sun, Moon, and Stars

When the fourth angel blows the Fourth Trumpet, one-third of
the sun, moon, and stars will grow dark, as is plainly predicted in
Revelation 8:12.

Again, what does he (John of Patmos, the author of Revelation)
mean by "one-third"? One-third of the total number of stars, or
one-third of each individual star? Look, who cares? The stars,
although very pretty, don't affect our lives the way the sun does.
(Neither does the moon's light, really — the moon causes tides,
but its brightness isn't that important.)

But when one-third of the sun grows dark, that *will* be bad.
Forget "global warming." Overnight we will experience "global
cooling," "global darkening," and "global being-depressed."
The whole world will be like Norway in the winter (and God
knows what Norway will be like). That's why we suggest selling any investment instrument you have left. Life as we know
it is coming to an end. Companies, corporations, stocks, equities — it's all "toast."

How can you make money in such a context? By turning to a
business technique adapted from life as we *used to* know it.

Get Pushy

When earthquakes and meteors and rampaging armies destroy farmland and processing factories and highways and trucks, how will people get food?

From you.

If you're looking for a way to earn some extra "income" (whether in the form of money, bottles of scotch, bags of potatoes, or ammunition), and if you're reasonably ambulatory, we have an exciting new way to put you in the fresh food–distribution business overnight.

🐷 MIND YOUR OWN BUSINESS

- You call it: On the Wagon
- You sell: Fresh, or at least fresh enough, produce
- You offer: Neighborhood delivery and an old-fashioned, "Lower East Side" atmosphere

Here's how:

1. Find an old trailer or U-Haul van.
2. Disassemble it to construct a large, flat, open cart capable of transporting several hundred pounds. Make sure the platform has sides to keep the cargo from sliding off.
3. Attach two parallel arms to the rear, for pulling the cart.
4. Scavenge abandoned homes, gardens, and markets for any remotely edible fruits and vegetables. (And don't forget to check abandoned restaurants.) Pile them on the cart.

---

5. Make the rounds of your neighborhood or what's left of it, announcing your arrival in a loud, clear voice, and maybe proclaiming what "specials" you have today. Then stand back as the customer traffic comes to *you*.

And there you have it. Minimal expense, no pricey (or nonexistent) gasoline, nonpolluting, and actually a source of healthful exercise. Who needs an industrial civilization?

FEARFULLY ASKED QUESTIONS (FAQ)

Q. I'm interested in starting a produce delivery service like the one you describe. But I'm not strong enough to push a cart myself. Where can I get an ox?

A. Ask around for recommendations for a good local ox man. If there aren't any in your general vicinity, you may have to try ordering over the Internet or by catalogue.

Q. Are tax-free municipal bonds a good investment for persons on a fixed income?

A. Sorry, there's no municipal anything anymore. Which trumpet did we lose you at?

Q. This is all very interesting, but I miss the Antichrist. Is he still around? What's he doing, and when will we see him again?

A. He is still around and busier than ever. Remember, not only does he have his hands full oppressing mankind as the Antichrist but, being indwelled by Satan, he has *that* whole thing to deal with. And, like everyone else, he has to navigate among the earthquakes and meteors, the falling Wormwood star, the moving mountains and islands, and the darkening of the heavenly bodies. He'll reappear soon, though — and when he does, look out!

CHAPTER 18

The Warning Angel and the Fifth Trumpet

Locusts from the Bottomless Pit

> In Heaven, an angel will announce to all present the terrible
> things that are about to be unleashed in the next three trumpet
> blasts, as noted in Revelation 8:13. These next three Trumpet
> Judgments are known as the Three Woes.

This happens in Heaven. Just forget about it. You'll have plenty
to deal with without having to worry about what angels are saying to one another.

> The first woe will arrive when a "star," which is referred to as
> "he" and "him," falls to the Earth. This star has "the key" to "the
> bottomless pit." He opens the pit, and huge billows of smoke
> come out, blocking the sun and fouling the air. Then a horrible
> swarm of special locusts will come out and torment all those
> without the mark of God on their foreheads. This will last for five
> months. It's all predicted in Revelation 9:1–11.

You may be surprised to learn that the Abyss (or "bottomless
pit") is not Hell. We certainly were. Everyone says "Go to Hell,"
but people rarely say "Go jump in the Abyss." Anyway, it seems to
be a place where evil spirits (or at least evil locusts) are imprisoned
until their day of judgment—or, apparently, until now, when they

will be unleashed to torment man. The description in Revelation 9:7–10 of these locusts specifies these unique characteristics:

* They will be shaped like horses.
* They will appear to be wearing golden crowns.
* They will have the faces of men.
* They will have the hair of women.
* They will have the teeth of lions.
* They will wear iron breastplates.
* There will be stings in their tails, like scorpions' tails.

We are told that, unlike ordinary locusts, these locusts will not damage plants or grass or anything green. Of course, that's cold comfort, considering that a third of the trees and all of the grass will have already been burned up by the hail and fire of the First Trumpet Judgment. In any case, the locusts will use their tails to sting people who have rejected God, causing a painful torment that will last for five months.

To make matters worse, Tim LaHaye says that these creatures "will not be observed by the human eye." That's right—they'll be invisible.

ARTIST'S RENDERING: INVISIBLE LOCUSTS OF THE FIFTH TRUMPET

LaHaye calls them "a spirit creature able to effect a physical response on humanity." Their king, the "angel of the bottomless pit," is named Abaddon in Hebrew and Apollyon in Greek. That may be useful to know, in case their master arrives to supervise them. Of course, unless you speak Hebrew or Greek, all you'll be able to do is call his name and get his attention, which may not be such a good idea after all.

For a graphic depiction of these locusts, see the "Artist's Rendering" on the previous page.

Knock Knock Knockin' on Customers' Doors

Once the invisible locusts arrive, people are *really* not going to want to go outside for any reason whatsoever. If you've decided to push a cart of produce around the neighborhood, this will unfortunately cut into your foot traffic. (It might also expose you to dangerous locust attacks.) And even if people do occasionally make a run for it from their homes to their cars (if they have gas), to get to some emergency destination like a hospital (if there are any still in operation), the last thing they're going to want to do is stop by your cart and inspect your bananas and onions.

Solution: You go to them. They may not want to come outside, but they should be willing to at least open the front door, grab you by the shirt, and drag you in as they slam the door shut.

Why should they? Because you're going to do this:

🐷 MIND YOUR OWN BUSINESS

- You call it: Kraig's List
- You sell: Anything you can get your hands on and transport
- You offer: Door-to-door service, and the pleasures of "impulse buying"

If the locusts are keeping people indoors, or if you just can't find any abandoned produce, here's an alternative retail strategy. All it requires of you is some energy, some resourcefulness, and the willingness to dodge invisible demons as you go about your business.

1. Roam the neighborhood and scavenge anything left that could possibly be of interest to anyone: appliances, toys, books, pillows, prescription drugs, kitchenware, clothing, shoes, weapons, et cetera. (These can of course include your old produce line.) Load them all onto a single, easily transportable means of conveyance, such as your converted U-Haul wagon or even a supermarket cart.

2. As you select each item, make a note of it.

3. If you have a wind-up computer or a battery-powered typewriter, or a piece of paper and a writing implement, compile a legible roster of the items, perhaps organized by use. *Do not specify any prices on the list.*

4. Push the cart from house to house. Park it as close as possible to the front doors.

5. Ring the bell or knock. When someone inside asks, "Who is it?" you call out, "Kraig!"

6. If they open the door, hand them a roster of your items. Introduce yourself as Kraig and identify the printout as Kraig's List.

7. If they fail to open the door, call out, "Kraig's List!" and shove the list in the mail slot or under the door.

8. If they invite or drag you in, go. If not, try to engage them in conversation in the doorway. Talk up your goods and make sure the customer realizes that you probably have *something* he needs or wants.

9. Negotiate prices for the items as you see fit. Remember, you paid nothing for them. Anything you get is profit.

(People have asked us whether it is necessary to call yourself Kraig and call your operation Kraig's List. We think it is. The original Craig's List will have been, by the time the Internet collapses during the Tribulation, a once-beloved online sales and contact site in cities all over the world. It will still possess what we call "name recognition." If we went from door to door offering "Steve and Evie Levy's List," we don't think we'd get many takers. With "Kraig," you at least stand a chance. Note that we spell it with a *K* to forestall any legal difficulties with the actual Craig.)

Typical Kraig's List house call. Note the salesman's vest and tie — even during the Tribulation, appearance counts.

CHAPTER 19

The Sixth Trumpet

An Army of 200,000,000 Horsemen Out of the East
Kills One-Third of Mankind

The Sixth Trumpet introduces the Second Woe: the release of four angels. These angels are presumably evil, because they have been "bound in the great river Euphrates" until this very moment. They take an hour, a day, a month, and a year to prepare, and then lead a terrible assault against mankind at the head of an army of two hundred million "horsemen." All this is predicted in detail in Revelation 9:13–19 (*14: Saying to the sixth angel which had the trumpet, Loose the four angels which are bound in the great river Euphrates. 15: And the four angels were loosed, which were prepared for an hour, and a day, and a month, and a year, for to slay the third part of men*).

The fact that the four angels take thirteen months and twenty-five hours to get started threatens to throw off the entire trumpet timetable, but maybe our calculations are wrong. Or maybe God will stop the clock until they're ready.

We're also not sure how these angels are going to recruit their army. For example, it's not clear whether these "horsemen" are actually men, and if their horses are actually horses. It doesn't sound like it: The horses have the heads of lions, and their mouths emit fire, smoke, and brimstone. (Brimstone is sulfur.) Even the

Typical horseman of the army of 200,000,000, on typical lion-headed, snake-tailed horse

tails of these "horses" are dangerous—they're like snakes, with heads and everything.

As implausible as this sounds, remember: It's the Bible, so it must be true. The important thing is that we try to get ready for what these horsemen are going to do, which is kill one-third of remaining humanity.

Now, remember that one-fourth of the world's population will have already *been* killed by the Fourth Horseman of the Apocalypse. Plus untold millions more will have been killed by various other calamities. Then the Sixth Trumpet will announce the killing of a third of whoever has survived.

Our figures place the maximum number of surviving humans

at around 2,565,891,800. Which is not to say that the glass is half full, by any means. But at least there's still a glass.

Teaching Teachers to Teach

You know the old saying "Those who can, do. Those who can't, teach."

We think that's just wrong. We think it should go "Those who can, do. Then, after they do, they should teach. And they shouldn't just teach what they can do, but also teach how to teach what they can do, too."

What with the onslaught of the invisible locusts and, now, the rampage of the 200,000,000-man army of Men on Lion-Headed Horses, people everywhere will be looking for new ways to make ends meet, for alternative revenue streams, or simply for a way to get their hands on something that they can trade for a half-dozen eggs and maybe a couple of English muffins.

If you've followed the advice we gave earlier and explored the new businesses we described, you will now possess certain things that such people will find increasingly valuable: knowledge and experience. So put them to work by selling them to others. Here's how.

🐷 MIND YOUR OWN BUSINESS

- You call it: (*Your Name*), Inc.
- You sell: Instruction and consultation
- You offer: The fruits of your experience and wisdom

Any or all of the businesses we've discussed previously can provide an ideal basis for an additional career as a teacher-consultant. Thus:

1. Viaticals: You can teach someone how to invest in viaticals, of course. But why stop there? Become a **viatical consultant**. Don't just offer instruction; sell your **ongoing advisory services** to anyone interested. And if potential customers hesitate, offer a money-back guarantee: If they don't get results within, say, a month of graduating your course, they'll get a full refund. Just remember to specify that the refund will be paid out in installments over two years. *Then make a viatical out of that.* Offer to buy them out now at a discount. They'll take a fraction of the refund and you'll have gotten off cheap.

2. Micro-Futures: Selling micro-futures (such as shares in a big can of beans or whatever that you open on a specified date in the future) involves a lot of organization and a bit of technical and legal work. That makes it great for **franchising**. Patent your own particular method and sell the whole package as a "turnkey" setup: *You* supply (at a markup) the big can of tomatoes (or tuna, juice, et cetera), the printed shares, the advertising, and so on. Then make all franchises use your futures exchange for their transactions. You get a cut, not only of every trade of *your* shares in the secondary market, but of theirs, too. Sweet!

3. Pushcarts: Sure, you can franchise your pushcart operation. But the burden of worrying about all those vendors, all that inventory, all that rolling stock—who needs it? Instead, offer **franchise consultancy** and teach others how to franchise their own similar operations. Let *them* go out into the field and deal with all those roaming gangs of looters, New Satanists, Antichrist field agents, horsemen, locusts, and whatever. You stay home, where it's (relatively) safe.

4. Kraig's List: Each "Kraig" will be an independent operator who will put together his or her own cart, stuff, and list. They won't be very sympathetic to centralized control or instruction. So forget selling any consultation services with these people. However, all the "Kraigs" out there will need one thing they won't be able to provide for themselves: inspiration! That's why you should be able to do a brisk business in **motivational speaking**. Give lectures, group exercises, retreats, and symposia. Make these various "Kraigs" "see" the vision you "saw" when you created the first Kraig's List.

5. Multilevel Marketing (MLM): As we noted earlier, MLM will be hot. And, because it involves a lot of people, networks, communication, and inventory, it's a natural for franchising — which means that everyone will want to franchise his or her own special MLM method. Inevitably, then, consulting about MLM franchises will be hot, too. That's where you fit in, when you become an MLM **franchise consultant consultant-franchiser.** You offer consultations about how to consult about how to start a franchise. And then franchise your consultancy operation and offer consultation to your own franchisees about how to consult *with you* about the franchises they're already consulting with you about!

As you can see, it may be the end of the world, but it doesn't have to be the end of capitalism, thanks to the energy, the courage, the creative resourcefulness, and the resourceful creativity of whoever seizes the opportunities listed above.

CHAPTER 20

Death and Resurrection of the Two Witnesses Prior to the Seventh Trumpet

After preaching for three and a half years, the Two Witnesses who appeared earlier (Elijah and, probably, Moses) will be killed by the Beast from the Bottomless Pit, or the Abyss. Their bodies will lie in plain view, in the streets of Jerusalem, for three and a half days. No one will bury or otherwise attend to them; on the contrary, people around the world, wallowing in their own wickedness and sin, will rejoice in the deaths and throw parties and exchange gifts. All of this is set forth plainly in Revelation 11:7–10.

Finally, after three and a half days, the Spirit of Life will enter the deceased witnesses. The whole world will watch as they come back to life. Then a voice in Heaven will summon them up, and they will ascend into the clouds. We learn this from Revelation 11:11–12 (*11: And after three days and an half the spirit of life from God entered into them, and they stood upon their feet; and great fear fell upon them which saw them. 12: And they heard a great voice from heaven saying unto them, Come up hither. And they ascended up to heaven in a cloud; and their enemies beheld them*).

We're not sure whether this will take place in Jerusalem or in Rome. We do know, however, that the Beast from the Abyss is the Antichrist. How can we be so certain? First, because the witnesses will have been preaching explicitly against the words and deeds of the Antichrist all this time, alienating and enraging him. Second, because it will take someone with the Antichrist's special powers (since he is now indwelled by Satan) to overcome the witnesses' ability to, among other things, spew fire from their mouths.

At this point the Trumpet Judgments are effectively over, but the global nightmare of the Day of the Lord is not. The Seventh Trumpet will cue the Bowl Judgments, which will of course be horrific. That's the bad news.

The good news is that as the bodies of Elijah and (probably) Moses lie untended-to in the streets of Jerusalem for three and a half days, people will start inviting you to parties and giving you presents in celebration! Plus, we are only about thirty days away

Gift-giving and rejoicing at the death of Elijah and, probably, Moses

from the end of the Tribulation. That means we have just about a month to get ready for the Second Coming.

Other good news—well, not "good," but certainly interesting—is that the ascension to Heaven of the dead witnesses will take place in view of the world. When you see it (since you will; it will presumably be televised), we suggest you start to think about dedicating what little time remains to—at last!—retirement.

To that end, let's update your portfolio in preparation for your "golden month."

Finance/Portfolio Update

If you've taken our advice, you've sold all your equities. You're sitting on a lot of cash. As soon as you see the witnesses rise up to Heaven:

1. Put all cash in a checking account and use its debit card for everything. Pay off your credit card debt, if the credit card companies still exist.
2. Sell all real estate (land and structures), collectibles, cars, jewelry, gold, silver, and artworks you have left. *Do not sell wine. Drink it or trade it for beer, scotch, vodka, et cetera.*
3. Stockpile the following items (see the pie graph on the next page). Adjust the approximate proportions illustrated to suit your particular lifestyle.
4. Use the land mines to secure your home or, in cooperation with any other tenants left alive, your apartment building. Use the other weapons to defend yourself and your family as the social order completely breaks down and your neighborhood starts to look like a cross between *The Road Warrior* and *Night of the Living Dead*.
5. Hunker down, stay inside, and enjoy your new home entertain-

BOWL JUDGMENT STOCKPILE: RIDING OUT THE LAST MONTH

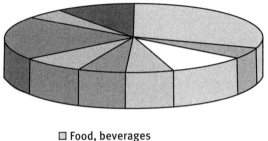

☐ Food, beverages
◩ Land mines
☐ Drugs, medical supplies
◩ Sidearms
▣ Automatic weapons
◩ RPGs, flamethrowers, etc.
▣ Home entertainment system
◩ DVDs, CDs, etc.
▣ Generator, fuel

ment system. Tip: In any music system, about half your budget should be spent on speakers. Don't "save money" on no-name "bargains." You get what you pay for! (And don't worry about overpriced high-end cables and interconnects. The sonic differences they make, if any, will be inaudible to anyone whose ears have made it through the Tribulation thus far.)

6. Get ready to retire in style! (See part V.)

Of course, it's possible you haven't taken our advice, and are still carrying (and even adding to) your credit card debt. We have a thought about that.

WWJC?*
(*WHAT WOULD JESUS CHARGE?)

Remember that Jesus is coming in about thirty days.

At this late date, it's hard to predict which merchants and dealers will still take credit cards. Some may. Some may take just cash. Still others, when you walk in the door, may assume you're a looter and shoot you on sight.

In any case, if you can still buy stuff with "plastic," you may be tempted to max out all your cards now, on the assumption that you'll get a "free ride" once Christ establishes His Kingdom on Earth, and not have to pay them off.

We call this "bankruptcy by salvation" and, frankly, we don't think it will work. True, Jesus may not be too crazy about the idea of charging interest, but we also believe He'll rule that a deal is a deal, and force everyone to pay off their credit card balances.

You can take the chance that He'll forgive your debts, but don't count on it. We think that, for Jesus as well as everyone else, God is love, but business is business.

CHAPTER 21

Earthquake Strikes Jerusalem, and the Seventh Trumpet

Remember when, at the opening of the First Seal, Israel got trendy and "hot" and you really wanted to move there? Now you can be glad you couldn't afford to.

> After the terrible treatment of the Two Witnesses by the residents of Jerusalem, God will send a massive earthquake to devastate the city. Once it's over, the survivors will "give glory" to God. This is set forth in Revelation 11:13 (*And the same hour was there a great earthquake, and the tenth part of the city fell, and in the earthquake were slain of men seven thousand: and the remnant were affrighted, and gave glory to the God of heaven*).

We'll be surprised, frankly, if this even makes the news. Only one-tenth of Jerusalem will collapse, and a mere seven thousand people will be killed. Maybe that's why people will give glory to God. They'll be thanking Him for letting them off easy.

If so, their gratitude will be short-lived. God is about to cue the Seventh Trumpet and, with it, the Bowl Judgments.

Time Out of Your Mind

> When the seventh angel sounds the Seventh Trumpet, there will be loud voices in Heaven proclaiming Christ's reign on Earth forever and ever, as noted in Revelation 11:15.

We wouldn't be surprised if these heavenly voices also took a moment to protest the confusing chronology of this part of the Tribulation. For example, chapter 13 in Revelation (two chapters after the passage about the Seventh Trumpet, above) *introduces* the Antichrist—the figure we've been living with and terrified of for at least three and a half years already. Later in chapter 13 we meet the False Prophet—whom, you will recall, we met in part III, chapter 2 of this book, way back at the opening of the First Seal.

Revelation chapter 14 introduces another 144,000 servants, whose identities are the subject of much dispute and who either are or are not the same people as the 144,000 proselytizing Jewish virgins. Revelation 15 brings forward the seven angels with their seven bowls, which makes sense, but then talks about God's "victory over the beast, and over his image, and over his mark, and over the number of his name." Since the beast is the Antichrist, and that victory won't happen for several chapters (and years), we're back into a confusing chronology again. It's not until Revelation 16 that we encounter the Bowl Judgments and get back on track in terms of sequence.

We're not afraid to make certain financial suggestions others might consider to be "unorthodox" or "high risk." But even we can't figure out how to make money off an agenda that praises events that haven't happened yet and introduces figures we met three years earlier. So let's just move on.

Part V The Tribulation: The Bowl Judgments

CHAPTER 22

The First Bowl

Sores on Men with the Mark of the Beast

With the blowing of the Seventh Trumpet comes the Third Woe, in the form of the terrible Bowl Judgments. Seven angels will appear in Heaven carrying seven "vials" (or bowls) full of the wrath of God. These seven judgments will express the Lord's extreme anger at all those who have not accepted Jesus as their savior. God, we're told, will want to rid the Earth of incorrigibles and unregenerate sinners, who will be unfit to live in the earthly paradise that will be set up in a few weeks. He will also be expressing His fury at "the nations" for their persecution of Israel throughout history and even into the Tribulation.

By the time the Bowl Judgments have run their course, the Earth will be in ruins and, if all goes according to our Heavenly Father's plan (which, by definition, it will), that should leave us with around five billion people killed and around one billion still alive—although "alive" does not necessarily mean "not injured," "not crippled," "not brain damaged," "not comatose," and "not driven crazy."

Still, if you're alive and in decent health, and if you've pursued any of the business options we outlined earlier, you're probably sitting on enough cash and goods to get through the next month in style and comfort. So let's talk more about that retirement!

> When the first angel pours out his bowl, sores will break out on those who have taken the Mark® of the Antichrist and who have chosen to worship him, as is foretold in Revelation 16:2.

Bad news for Take Its: Here is where you get caught. We don't know exactly what Revelation means when it says you're going to come down with a "grievous sore," and we're not sure we want to know.

Still, even Take Its, sores and all—along with those Fake Its and Forsake Its who managed to outwit either the Antichrist or God or both—can look forward to a happy and productive retirement lasting well into the next month.

But retirement during the period of the Bowl Judgments will involve more than just sleeping in and then puttering around in the remains of the workshop all day, or playing imaginary golf, or searching for potable water. You might need to acquaint yourself with a new set of ideas and a new range of skills with which to meet the challenges of the final weeks of the Tribulation.

To see if you're prepared for those challenges, we've devised a test. Answer the following questions about your financial and living habits as they are *now*. Then calculate your score to determine whether you are or aren't "retirement ready."

READER SELF-ASSESSMENT: ARE YOU BOWL-JUDGMENT, PRE–SECOND COMING, RETIREMENT READY?

Answer True or False

1. I am alive. **T F**
2. I have a financial record-keeping system on a piece of paper in my shoe that can accompany me to wherever I flee. **T F**

3. My daily weekday routine involves going to an office and not being kidnapped en route. **T F**

4. My daily weekday routine involves hiding in a basement. **T F**

5. I have a household spending plan or budget that I adhere to rigorously and that includes substantial disbursements for weapons and painkillers. **T F**

6. I have a predictable income stream that includes the commission of armed robbery. **T F**

7. Every year I contribute to a "Christmas Club" fund until I have saved enough to buy a club with which to protect myself during the holidays. **T F**

8. When necessary, I can enjoy a complete physical "workout" in my closet. **T F**

9. I have at least one hobby in addition to foraging. **T F**

10. I have an emergency fund that covers three to six months of my living expenses, including payments for bribes, assassinations, and "protection." **T F**

11. I consider a shoe box to be a low-risk savings account. **T F**

12. Each year I review my annual Social Security statement and burst into tears. **T F**

13. I don't dip into my retirement savings unless a duly authorized public official requests that I do so or he will kill my family. **T F**

14. I have a living will or, if not, at least I have the will to live. **T F**

15. I have adequate life insurance, and I keep it well-oiled with the safety on. **T F**

16. I have explored the pros and cons of long-term-care insurance and have concluded the hell with it. **T F**

17. For maximum return on my investments I have invested in no-load mutual funds and/or tax-free municipal bonds and/or US savings bonds before liquidating everything and putting it into chips at the Bellagio in Vegas. **T F**

18. I have searched to find the lowest interest rates and fees on a home mortgage and am certain that they are expressible and payable in cans of Beefaroni. **T F**

19. I have, in ways not relevant to this discussion, acquired a substantial hoard of Beefaroni. **T F**

20. I have calculated how much money I will need for retirement, *and* I have adjusted my savings plan, my budget, my income, and my lifestyle to ensure that I will reach my retirement goals, *and* I am certain that in fact I will reach those goals in spite of anything that happens in the outside world, because I know exactly how long I am going to live, and because I am insane. **T F**

Scoring: Award yourself one point for every True (T) answer.

WHAT YOUR SCORE MEANS:

15–20 points: You're not only ready to retire, you may actually survive!

10–14 points: You're in good shape. Just be sure there's enough food and ammunition for you and your children.

5–9 points: You have a way to go. To build up your retirement resources, consider selling some major asset, such as a kidney.

0–4 points: You are simply not ready to retire yet. Good luck.

CHAPTER 23

The Second Bowl

The Seas Turn to Blood. All Creatures in the Sea Die

When the second angel pours out the Second Bowl of wrath, all the oceans and seas of the world will turn completely to blood, as is foretold in Revelation 16:3 (*And the second angel poured out his vial upon the sea; and it became as the blood of a dead man: and every living soul died in the sea*).

Remember how, with the Second Trumpet, one-third of the Mediterranean turned to blood? Now the rest of it (and perhaps all the other seas and oceans) will, too. We don't know what the blood type will be, probably because this prediction was written between AD 68 and 96, before they knew what *blood type* (or *circulatory system*) meant. But we do know that it will happen.

Say every sea turns to blood. Assuming the moon stays where it is (despite also being blood—in color, at least), the oceans will continue to have tides, so the oceans-of-blood will have at least a little bit of movement. Yes, the specific gravity of blood is higher than that of even ocean water, but just never mind. The point is this: What about the smaller lakes and ponds? Are they "seas"? Will they clot? The Bible doesn't say.

But it does say that all marine life—animals, anyway; who knows if plants have "living souls"?—will die. The oceans will become huge sludge pools of decaying fish and sea-dwelling mammals. Presumably a lot of birds who feed on fish will die, too. Tim LaHaye explains how serious this is when he writes, "This judgment may well interfere with commercial shipping and send whole populations into confusion as people grope for an adequate supply of water, not to mention destroying what is left of the fish industry."

A Place In, or Better Yet Not In, the Sun

Where will you live when you retire?

For many people the answer (until the Rapture occurs) would have been some sort of retirement community. Over the past fifty years, hundreds of such developments have opened, catering to a wide range of retirees' needs and desires. From living on a golf course to living near a lake on a golf course, from living in the mountains surrounded by golf courses to living on the beach but never going to it but instead spending all your time on the golf course, retirement communities for "active adults" have offered amenities and golf courses for every lifestyle.

Retirement during the final period of the Bowl Judgments will (aside from the seas' and oceans' being blood) be no different, except for the golf courses. There won't be any. At least there won't be any made of grass, although retirement community developers like Dwell Ebb might be able to figure out a cost-effective way to replace the world's burned-up fairways and greens with Astroturf. Then again, how many people will want to remain outside for however long it takes to play golf, in plain view on an open fairway, as easy targets for marauding armies, roving criminal gangs, and falling meteors? And all those pretty ponds and pools that decorate golf courses? They're now blood hazards.

But it doesn't matter. There are many other kinds of retirement communities specifically designed for the unique challenges of life during the End Times. Some are nearing completion, while others are still closer to the planning stages. We offer a sample in the chart below.

END TIMES RETIREMENT COMMUNITIES

Name of Community	Location	Offerings, Amenities, and Special Events	The Lure of the Area	Lifestyle Philosophy
Heresy Estates	Hades Lake, AZ	Group sex, child sacrifices, Black Mass every Sunday, wi-fi	Friendly, warm neighbors who keep their mouths shut and don't ask questions	"There is no God but Satan, and the Antichrist is his messenger."
The Redoubt at Citadel Tor	Endless Vista, WY	Each street is gated, walled, moated, and domed. Motion detectors on every lamppost. Proprietary "Floating Land Mines"™ around perimeter of each home.	Wide-open, highly defensible spaces. Clear firing lines. "No-fly" airspace zoning.	"Maximum security for an unsurpassed quality, or at least quantity, of life."
Mesa-on-the-Glen-by-the-Sea-Near-the-Beach	Cape Adorable, NC	Arts and crafts center, weekly Hummel/Lladro gymkhana, competitive knitting league, annual Pro-Am Pysanky Egg Throwdown	Area craft stores deliver. Local species of chipmunks and squirrels not yet extinct.	"Stay safe. Stay inside. Enjoy the Cute Life™—and stay alive."
Mini-Links Manor	Bush, CO	Condos and homes built on and around five "fully carpeted" miniature golf courses. Single-family units actually shaped like course hazards ("Fairy Tale Castle," "Dutch Windmill," "Ferris Wheel," etc.).	Not applicable. Entire community—golf courses, homes, rec center, shops, schools, medical offices, police, etc.—is enclosed inside a giant warehouse.	"All You Need Is a Putter—and a Dream."

CONTINUED ON NEXT PAGE

CONTINUED FROM PREVIOUS PAGE

Name of Community	Location	Offerings, Amenities, and Special Events	The Lure of the Area	Lifestyle Philosophy
The Legacy Villages of Dagnabbit Falls	Consarned-All-Getout, MO	Traditional Americana lifestyle: whittling, yarn-spinning, harmless joshing, telling fish stories, egg-and-spoon racing, apple-bobbing, hay rides, ice cream socials, cannonballs at the swimming hole, ham-and-clam church picnics, pie-eating contests, kids sassing their elders, young folks courting and sparking, covered-dish get-togethers, brass band concerts at the gazebo, softball games on the Fourth of July, kissing booths at the Founders' Day Carnival, Christmas carols, sleigh rides, inexplicable, brutal murder-suicides of entire families	No Jews, Muslims, Buddhists, Hindus, or Catholics	"We Pretend Like It's 1904 Because That's What God Prefers."

FEARFULLY ASKED QUESTIONS (FAQ)

Q. My husband and I are concerned about the environment. Are there any "eco-friendly" retirement communities that will be available during the Tribulation? Can we "retire green" until Jesus comes?

A. Since the purpose of the Tribulation is pretty much the destruction of all plant, animal, and human life on Earth except for those Christians who accept Jesus, it's not clear what being "eco-friendly" will mean. There really won't be any "eco" left to be friendly *to*. However, we understand that StoneDance Ranch in Flinkk, Montana, will be a "geo-friendly" community, in which residents will be encouraged to express and to share with one another their respect for and kindness to rocks.

Q. What are derivatives?

A. It doesn't matter what derivatives are at this point. Why didn't you ask us in part III, during the Seal Judgments? We could have helped you then. Now, forget it.

CHAPTER 24

The Third Bowl
Rivers and Springs Become Blood

As a sort of "sequel" to the Second Bowl, the pouring of the Third Bowl will turn anything remaining of the Earth's natural water supply into blood, as foretold in Revelation 16:4 (*4: And the third angel poured out his vial upon the rivers and fountains of waters; and they became blood*). This will be followed by an approving reaction to it and an explanation of its rationale in Revelation 16:5–6 (*5: And I heard the angel of the waters say, Thou art righteous, O Lord, which art, and wast, and shalt be, because thou hast judged thus. 6: For they have shed the blood of saints and prophets, and thou hast given them blood to drink*).

This judgment "pays back" the Antichrist for shedding the blood of so many martyred Christians. Now he and all remaining nonbelievers will have only blood to drink. It also seems to satisfy the Tribulation martyrs who, earlier, were under the altar in Heaven, complaining to God (in Revelation 6:9–10) about when He was going to avenge their murders.

Caveat Investor

Unfortunately, retirees make especially tempting targets for fraud. And the Tribulation will only exacerbate this problem.

Perpetrators of scams assume—often correctly—that retired people are cash rich and savvy poor, that they're naive when it comes to the Internet, and that they possess a lot of free time in which to pursue various get-rich-quick schemes.

Not surprisingly, this trend will only get worse as the Tribulation unfolds and more and more people get increasingly desperate about money, safety, and survival. That's why we want you to beware of deceptions like these:

Classic Scams Aimed at Retirees

1. "The Raptured Nigerian": You receive an e-mail or, if the Internet no longer works, a carrier pigeon from an official (or "the widow" of an official) in the Nigerian government, claiming that a bank account containing $23.5 million (US) has been abandoned after its owner "was Raptured unto Heaven by Our Lord Jesus Christ." The message asks that you help the sender smuggle the money out of Nigeria (and into your own bank account), at which point you will receive a percentage of the take. Then, when you agree, the sender asks that you mail a six-pack of canned chili for use in bribing corrupt Nigerian officials. However, once you send the chili, you never hear from him or her again.

2. "The Food Inspector": Someone comes to your door claiming to be an "inspector" from "the government Pure Food Department." He asks if you have any food in the house. When you say yes, he asks what it is. When you tell him, he says that he has been sent to assure that your food isn't poisoned or contaminated. He will ask to inspect it. When you give it to him, he will eat it, then confirm that it was indeed safe. He may then issue you a fake "certificate of purity" before he leaves.

3. "Identity Mugging": A couple comes to your door and claims that they are you and your spouse. After all, they know your name and, obviously, your address. They insist you leave "their" home or they will call the police. Because you (a) are retired, and therefore probably middle-aged or older, and (b) have been through almost seven years of unmitigated hell since the Rapture, by now you doubt your own sanity. And, since no one except a lunatic would make such an outlandish claim falsely, you decide that they must be right — they are you, and you and your spouse must be someone else and someone else's spouse. You apologize and leave. Only later, after friends and neighbors greet you as yourself, does it dawn on you that they may have been lying. By then they have eaten all your food and escaped.

4. "The Affinity Ruse": As the Tribulation proceeds, people will find solace, support, and consolation in new "affinity groups," i.e., organizations of like-minded individuals brought together by one specific interest. Affinity groups of a religious nature will flourish as people come together to express their resentment at not having been Raptured away and spared the Tribulation's agony. Particularly popular will be such organizations as Jews Against Jesus (angry Jews), the Young Men's Anti-Christian Association (ecumenical, nondenominational rage), and Opus Die (embittered Catholics). Perpetrators of cons will often take advantage of these new kinds of group loyalties in a scam that can take weeks or even months to unfold. The con becomes a member of the "mark's" organization and uses that as the basis to cultivate a friendship. Eventually so much trust and fellow feeling is built up that the mark thinks nothing of it when the con man suggests they have lunch or dinner together. They enjoy a pleasant meal, but when the check is presented, the con man "suddenly realizes" that he has no money. The unsuspecting mark volunteers to pick up the tab, assured that his deceiver will "get the next one."

But there is no next one. The free meal is what the con man had in mind all along, and the mark never hears from him again.

5. "Are You in God Hands?": Everyone knows that retirees have more problematic (and expensive) medical conditions than younger people. Health insurance can, therefore, be a matter of crucial importance. Combine that with the general perilous nature of the times and the heightened religious atmosphere, and you've got a formula for fraud. Thus, when a man wearing a suit and carrying a briefcase comes unexpectedly to your door, beware. He may cite an "appointment" you don't remember making. He'll then claim to be an insurance agent representing a number of different companies with "religiously certified" coverage, such as Mutual of Ohmigod or Jew Cross / Jew Shield. And all he'll require as a deposit on the policy is three apples or a (15 oz.) can of diced tomatoes. It almost sounds too good to be true. . . .

If it sounds too good to be true, it is. We urge our readers to be on the lookout for these and similar forms of deception, theft, and manipulation.

CHAPTER 25

The Fourth Bowl

The Sun Scorches the Earth

With the pouring of the Fourth Bowl, the sun will grow un-
bearably hot, burning men who, even then, will continue to
blaspheme and refuse to glorify God, as foretold in Revelation
16:8–9.

It's true that the sun was darkened by one-third during the Fourth
Trumpet Judgment, but that still leaves two-thirds of it for use in
the Fourth Bowl Judgment. Besides, when it comes to scorching
men with great heat, the Lord in His wisdom will presumably
know what He's doing. Remember, after the Third Bowl Judgment, men (and women, and kids) will have almost no access
to freshwater for cooling their bodies or quenching their thirst.
Sure, they can drink blood, but who wants to? Two-thirds of a
sun is all God will need to torment us in the service of His holy
plan.

Learn to Speak in Tongues

Even if the invisible locusts have gone elsewhere, some people
will want to stay inside as much as possible. And why not? For
one thing, the world will be filled with sunburned blasphemers,
and nobody wants to run into them. Plus, if you're retired, you're

not going to an office anymore. There will be no natural world left to enjoy and no swimming to be done in the bloody lakes, rivers, and oceans. There will be no sights left to see, almost no friends or loved ones left alive to visit, and, of course, no natural golf.

What will you sensible shut-ins do with your time? We suggest, among other things, that you learn some foreign languages. As we've said all along, barter will replace the use of money as a medium of exchange, and the odds are now good that you'll have to deal with people for whom English is not the primary tongue.

To get you started, we've created a chart showing how to say three things in three languages not commonly taught in US schools (Italian, Dutch, and Greek) that will be useful in your barter negotiations.

THREE USEFUL NEGOTIATING PHRASES
IN THREE FOREIGN LANGUAGES

Phrase	How to say it in Italian	How to say it in Dutch	How to say it in Greek
I will give you either five dollars or a bottle of French dressing if you stop eating my decorative cacti.	Vi darò cinque dollari o una bottiglia della preparazione francese se smettete di mangiare i miei cactus decorativi.	Ik zal u of vijf dollars of een fles van Franse vulling geven als u ophoudt etend mijn decoratieve cactussen.	Θα σας δώσω είτε πένε δολάρια είτε ένα μπουκάλι της γαλλικής σάλτσας εάν σταματήσετε τους διακοσμητικούς κάκτους μου.
I hope you enjoyed sleeping in my car. Now please give me the two Valiums and the box of Rice Krispies as we agreed.	Spero che abbiate goduto dormire in mio automobile. Ora vogliate mi danno i due Valiums e la scatola di riso Krispies come abbiamo accosentito.	Ik hoop u genoot van slaap in mijn auto. Nu te geven gelieve me twee Valiums en de doos Rijst Krispies aangezien wij akkoord gingen.	Ελπίζω ότι απολαύσατε στο αυτοκίνητό μου. Τώρα παρακαλώ μου δώστε τα δύο Valiums και το κιβώτιο του ρυζιού Krispies όπως συμφωνήσαμε.
A down parka for one of my kidneys? That is absurd.	Giù un parka per uno dei miei reni? Quello è irragionevole.	Een benedenparka voor één van mijn nieren? Dat is absurd.	Μια κάτω ζακέτα για ένα από τα νεφρά μου; Αυτός ειναι παράλογος.

Naturally, these three phrases won't be enough to deal with every negotiation you'll encounter from now until the Second Coming. (You may, for example, live in an apartment and not even have decorative cacti.) Therefore we encourage you to find new phrases to suit your particular lifestyle.

CHAPTER 26

The Fifth Bowl

The Kingdom of the Antichrist/Beast Becomes Full of Darkness

> The pouring of the Fifth Bowl will cause the city of Babylon to grow completely dark, prompting men to gnaw their tongues in frustration and misery. And yet they *still* will not repent! Instead, they'll continue to blaspheme and deny Christ. All this is predicted in Revelation 16:10–11 (*10: And the fifth angel poured out his vial upon the seat of the beast; and his kingdom was full of darkness, and they gnawed their tongues for pain, 11: And blasphemed the God of heaven because of their pains and their sores, and repented not of their deeds*).

This judgment concerns the place where the Antichrist will have his global headquarters: the rebuilt biblical city of Babylon, about sixty miles south of Baghdad.

Of course, today modern Babylon is kind of barren. There are a few of Saddam's big pretentious palaces (which house US military forces), a lot of rubble of interest to archaeologists, and some restored ruins, all surrounded by dirt roads, open plains, and dusty palm groves.

But the Antichrist will change all that. He'll make it the most fantastic city in the world and move his whole operation there (and all in about six years). As Tim LaHaye tells us, the ancient city will become "the center of all commerce, religion, evil, and government." Kind of like LA, Washington, DC, and New York City rolled into one!

Budget Travel: On the Road Again

We'd love to see Babylon in its revived, resplendent state. But by the time it reaches its apex (just before it goes dark), international travel will have become extremely difficult, expensive, and dangerous.

Still, other kinds of travel will be possible—and some at bargain prices. So, if you're one of those folks who absolutely must leave the house to explore the unknown, here's one itinerary suitable for almost any retiree's budget.

To start, you'll need this equipment:

✔ Two shoes (a left and a right) that fit reasonably well and, if possible, socks
✔ Long trousers (for men or women), plus a belt, rope, wire, duct tape, suspenders, or some other means of holding them up
✔ A shirt
✔ A thick, strong stick about four feet long
✔ A handgun or semiautomatic weapon
✔ A knapsack or canvas bag

Once you have these materials, follow the steps below. Feel free to improvise to suit your own interests and sense of adventure.

1. Put on the socks and shirt. Put on the trousers and hold them up with the belt, wire, or whatever. (Wear something comfortable, but be sure to show respect for local dress customs.) Put on the shoes.
2. Wear the knapsack on your back or sling the canvas bag over a shoulder.
3. Carry the big stick in one hand and the gun or semiautomatic in the other. (Be sure it's loaded.)

4. Go to the front door of your home, if you still have one. Open it and *go outside.*

Yes, it's scary. Yes, it's dangerous. That's the point. *Travel,* during the End Times, shouldn't mean just walking around your living room. *Adventure* has got to mean something beyond staring out the window and pretending you're in Italy. Or it shouldn't *only* mean that. It should also mean exposing yourself to new people, new risks, new experiences.

5. Walk to the edge of whatever street, highway, or road your home is on. Use the big stick for walking over rubble, clearing away obstacles, and beating off marauding gangs of attackers. Use the gun for this, too.
6. Make sure no car or horse traffic is coming, and then —
7. *Step out into the street.*

Now pause for a moment to appreciate just how different this "world" is from your home. At home, for example, you can see only scattered patches of blue sky through the holes in your ceilings and your roof. Outside, the sky, to the extent that it isn't obscured by the billowing smoke of fires and explosions, seems to go on forever.

8. Cross all the way to the *other side of the street.*

At this point you may happen to see other people. Feel free to greet or avoid or kill them, depending on their behavior and your personal "style."

9. Once across the street, look for some object or item (a "souvenir") worth keeping. Put it in your knapsack or bag.
10. Retrace your steps and bring the object *back to your home.*

Travel, toward the end of the Tribulation, will be as easy as stepping outside your front door.

Congratulations! You've taken about as ambitious and revivi-fying a trip as will be possible at this point in human history. No, it's not the same as shooting snapshots of Notre Dame or dancing the samba in Rio during *Carnaval* or breathing the air of the Grand Canal in Venice. Forget them. They're gone. We are nearing the end of the Tribulation. Crossing the street and living to tell about it will be enough adventure for anyone.

So enjoy every second of it. You'll not only have an impressive story to tell your friends and loved ones, if any remain alive, but you'll have proof of it.

Bon voyage. And good luck.

CHAPTER 27

The Sixth Bowl

The Euphrates River Dries Up

When the sixth angel pours out his bowl on the Euphrates, the river (which had previously been turned into blood) will dry up, preparing the way for the kings from the east to cross it en route to the Valley of Jezreel for the Battle of Armageddon. So predicts Revelation 16:12 (*And the sixth angel poured out his vial upon the great river Euphrates; and the water thereof was dried up, that the way of the kings of the east might be prepared*).

But then something changes. Revelation 16:13–14 introduces three froglike demons who seem to recruit the armies for a different purpose (*13: And I saw three unclean spirits like frogs come out of the mouth of the dragon, and out of the mouth of the beast, and out of the mouth of the false prophet. 14: For they are the spirits of devils, working miracles, which go forth unto the kings of the earth and of the whole world, to gather them to the battle of that great day of God Almighty*).

Why are these Asian kings and their armies gathered for battle in the first place? Plus, *are* there kings in Asia? We don't know. They may be amassed on the banks of the Euphrates in preparation for an attack on the forces of the Antichrist, headquartered in teeming, sinful, "happening" Babylon.

But that's not really news. What *is* news is that three froglike spirits will come out of the mouths of Satan, the Antichrist, and the False Prophet to lead a mighty army in battle against the forces of God and His Son, Jesus Christ.*

Money for Nothing

We've been saying all along that as the Day of the Lord proceeds, money will be less and less important as governments collapse and the world reverts to the barter system. Still, some people will continue to hoard notes and coins, and some will continue to accept them as legal tender.

What if you still have some money? What if, in your explorations of abandoned houses and wallets and purses, you've collected a lot? What should you spend it on?

If you've been saving for retirement for ten or twenty years or more, you probably fantasized about spending your money on these classic retirement activities:

1. Cruises
2. Culture (art shows, concerts, and theater)
3. Gardening
4. Biking
5. Boating

---

*It sounds crazy—to go willingly against the forces of God Himself! But Tim LaHaye reminds us that Reverend Clarence Larkin has addressed this very matter, in his study entitled The Book of Revelation. Reverend Larkin unforgettably asks, "If a religious fanaticism could, at nine different times, cause hundreds of thousands of religious devotees to undergo unspeakable hardships for a religious purpose, what will not the miracle-working wonders of the 'froglike demons' of the last days of this Dispensation not be able to do in arousing whole nations, and creating vast armies to march in all directions from all countries, headed by their Kings, for the purpose of preventing an establishment of the Kingdom of the King of Kings in his own Land of Palestine?"

We have no answer to that. All we know is that by the end of the Sixth Bowl Judgment the armies of the world, or at least a lot of them, will be amassed at Armageddon, and they will be led by three demons that look like frogs.

6. Antiquing
7. Woodworking
8. Entertaining
9. Painting pictures
10. Card and board games

It's a nice list. But forget it. None of these is going to be available or possible by the time those frog demons emerge from the mouths of the Unholy Trinity. Here, in highly summarized form, is why:

1. Cruises: The seas and oceans are blood and clogged with dead fish.
2. Culture: Who wants to "go out" and to see and be seen when everyone is a mess?
3. Gardening: How? There's no water in reservoirs or, presumably, from the skies. Any available bottled water anyone has must be conserved for human consumption. Plus, between the sun's turning dark and then getting hot, planting anything is a joke.
4. Biking: Where? Past destroyed buildings and dead bodies? So that feral gangs of hoodlums can attack you to steal your clothes? Please.
5. Boating: See "Cruises." But this would be worse because you're that much closer to the actual blood. And what are you going to use for gas?
6. Antiquing: It's doubtful anything really nice has survived almost seven years of earthquakes, war, meteors, and pillaging.
7. Woodworking: This may not be completely impossible, but with no trees, what are you going to make? A nice chest of drawers out of your old chest of drawers? As a handsome addition to your blasted den? You're better off making spears.

8. Entertaining: As in "inviting people over to give them food for free"? It goes without saying that this is completely out of the question.

9. Painting Pictures: Maybe. But you're faced with either doing it outside, surrounded by destruction and danger, or inside, and going even more stir-crazy than necessary.

10. Card and Board Games: This seems the least impractical of our top-ten list. If you can find three other people not too ill, depressed, or terrified to play bridge or Monopoly with, be our guest. Lose one card, though, and you're in trouble, since replacing, e.g., the six of clubs or St. James Place will be difficult if not impossible.

We know: It's a grim rundown. The Tribulation will have made impossible practically every pleasant retirement pastime known to humanity. But then, that's its purpose. And the only reason we omitted "playing with grandchildren" from the list is that we couldn't bring ourselves to even think about it.

Still, there's a bright side to all this. With the money you're not spending on retirement activities, you can afford to buy a really nice wedding present for Jesus when He gets married. So set aside that cash you planned to use to live "the good life," put it in a box, and keep reading.

CHAPTER 28

The Seventh Bowl

The Greatest Earthquake Ever. Spiritual Babylon Is Destroyed. Commercial Babylon Is Destroyed

At the emptying of the Seventh Bowl, a great voice will intone, "It is done," followed by thunder and lightning. Then there will be the largest earthquake in history. Islands will run away, and mountains will become lost or missing. Also, hailstones each weighing a "talent" (anywhere from 40 to, according to one book, 135 pounds) will fall upon men and, presumably, women and children. People will still blaspheme, however, because they'll be so mad about the gigantic hail. This is clearly predicted in Revelation 16:17–21.

The earthquake will also destroy "religious Babylon," a common End Times term that even our sources interpret symbolically. To them, "religious Babylon" means other, non-Christian and even non-Protestant religions. They point to Revelation 17:1–6 (*1: And there came one of the seven angels which had the seven vials, and talked with me, saying unto me, Come hither, I will shew unto thee the judgment of the great whore that sitteth upon many waters: 2: With whom the kings of the earth have committed fornication, and the inhabitants of the earth have been made drunk with the wine of her fornication*).

Apparently *this* "Babylon" refers not to the Iraqi city but to "the religious prostitute of Babylonian idolatry," which means all religions (including most Protestant sects and Catholicism) except Fundamentalist Dispensationalist Protestantism. With the pouring of the Seventh Bowl of God's wrath, most Protestants, all Catholics, and all non-Christians will be destroyed — whatever *destroyed* means. Will all Babylonian idolaters be killed? Good question.

"Commercial Babylon" will also be destroyed, as noted in Revelation 18:1–3.

Tim LaHaye says that in this case, "Babylon" *can* be interpreted literally. It means the actual city, which as we know will have become the center of the world. With its fall, the Bowl Judgments are over and the great climactic battle is about to take place.

But first, we have a confession to make. . . .

Part VI One Wedding and an Apocalypse

CHAPTER 29

Saved by the Bowl: A Confession

A t the beginning of this book we said we wouldn't be eligible for the Rapture. We said we'd be left behind along with our fellow Jews, plus the Catholics, most other Christian sects, the Muslims, Hindus, Buddhists, Taoists, and the members of all the other non-Christian religions who had not accepted Jesus as their personal savior and, for whatever reason, refused to take the Bible (both Old and New Testaments) literally. And we meant it.

But as we wrote the book, we began wondering: Once all these prophecies started coming true, and all these amazing, improbable, or downright "impossible" events began taking place, how could people—how could *we*—continue to doubt? Oh sure, at the beginning, with a few million people flying up into the air and a guy on a red horse riding around dispensing war, you could maybe laugh it off or explain it away. But what if the predictions kept coming true, right on schedule?

Wouldn't it, sooner or later, be obvious and indisputable that the Fundamentalist Dispensationalist Premillennialists were right *all along*? And that everyone else who ever lived during the entire history of the world (except for Daniel, Isaiah, Ezekiel, Zechariah, the apostles, and John of Patmos) was wrong?

So we came up with what we agreed was a reasonable set of

criteria. We decided that with the pouring of the Seventh Bowl in Heaven and after the mammoth earthquake and the destruction of spiritual and commercial Babylon — but not a minute before — we will accept Jesus as our personal savior, if we're still alive.

And this is not just to save our skins, as a ploy to get out of being cast into the Lake of Fire when the Final Judgment comes. We'll *really mean it.*

We know. You're surprised. So were we, when we first discussed it. But think about it. How many islands have to move about and rivers turn to blood before you have to admit that Revelation is right and *The Origin of Species* is wrong? How many froglike demons have to come out of Satan's mouth before you have to admit that any born again minister understands the universe better than Albert Einstein?

So we're ready to come to Jesus. Are we suggesting you do the same? Not at all. Believe us, we have no problem telling you what to do with your money. But your soul is another matter. All we can do is tell you what we will do when the time comes.

Being saved means that we'll be around for the events described in the following pages. When (SPOILER ALERT!) Satan's army is defeated at the Battle of Armageddon, we'll be here to glory in it along with everyone else. When Jesus establishes His Thousand-Year Reign on Earth, we'll be two of His subjects. When 20 billion people move into the 1,500-mile-high structure that is the New Jerusalem (after it descends from Heaven), we'll be among them.

It will, after the unfortunate consignment of most of our friends and loved ones to an eternity of hellish torment, be wonderful.

But first: a wedding!

CHAPTER 30

The Wedding of the Lamb

The Church refers to itself as the Bride of Christ, based on such writings as 2 Corinthians 11:2 (. . . *I have espoused you to one husband, that I may present you as a chaste virgin to Christ*). Now, prior to His Second Coming, Jesus will (in Heaven) take His bride to wed, as foretold in Revelation 19:7–8 (*7: Let us be glad and rejoice, and give honour to him: for the marriage of the Lamb is come, and his wife hath made herself ready*).

Do they really mean it? A *wedding* wedding? With receiving line and in-laws and a caterer and a band? Why not? God, Who can do anything He wants, can certainly throw a wedding for His Son, even though usually it's the bride's family that pays.

In this case, "the bride" is the Church, which consists of all the believers in Christ, from the day of Pentecost (when, fifty days after the Resurrection, the Holy Ghost appeared to the apostles) to the day of the Rapture. All of these people, residing in their soul bodies, will be in Heaven.

That means that, even though we will have been born again by accepting Jesus, we won't be invited (because we'll still be alive on Earth, not having been "saved" early enough to qualify for the Rapture). However, we'll still feel compelled to send over, or up, a little something to mark the occasion.

The Wedding of the Lamb (NB: Veils, clothes, etc. for illustrative
purposes only. Actual bride[s] will have "soul bodies" and wear white linen.
Bible does not say whether it will wrinkle.)

Maybe you should, too. That's why we advised you earlier to
take all the money you won't spend on retirement activities and
put it into a really nice wedding present for Jesus and the Church.
Don't worry about being "original" in your choice of gift. To the
best of our knowledge, they won't be registered anywhere, so inevitably there will be duplication.

There will also be widespread bafflement about what to buy.
After all, what kind of gift do you get a couple that includes several billion brides (all of whom are, technically, dead and many
of whom are male) and a groom who (a) has everything and
(b) doesn't want anything? But Jesus, more than most, knows
that "it's the thought that counts."

FEARFULLY ASKED QUESTIONS (FAQ)

Q. Will there be a reception after the wedding of the Lamb?

A. Yes, although the Bible doesn't describe it. Revelation 19:9 does tell us that there will be a marriage supper (*And he saith unto me, Write, Blessed are they which are called unto the marriage supper of the Lamb. And he saith unto me, These are the true sayings of God*). We know that John the Baptist will be there, since he is quoted in John 3:28–29 as comparing himself to a friend of a groom (*28: Ye yourselves bear me witness, that I said, I am not the Christ, but that I am sent before him. 29: He that hath the bride is the bridegroom: but the friend of the bridegroom, which standeth and heareth him, rejoiceth greatly because of the bridegroom's voice: this my joy therefore is fulfilled*).

Q. If I do buy Jesus a wedding gift, how do I get it to Him?

A. Presumably in a way similar to how children mail Christmas letters to Santa Claus. They simply write, "Santa Claus / North Pole," and the letter reaches the addressee. We think if you just address your gift "Jesus" and mail it, it will reach the intended recipient, assuming the postal system still exists.

Q. Will Jesus and His bride go on a honeymoon?

A. Yes. Although its description in Revelation 19:11 is kind of vague, Tim LaHaye assures us, "The earth — the former abode of the Church, from which the Church will have been raptured, and the place where the Lamb Himself lived and died — will then become the place of the thousand-year honeymoon. Would to God that every marriage could enjoy the fulfillment of that symbol — one thousand years of peace."

What can we add, except "Amen"?

Before the honeymoon, though, Jesus — like many busy grooms — will have some business to attend to. He'll be leading the armies of Heaven in a final confrontation with Evil. This is all the more reason why, when they get here, we should greet Jesus and His wife with the courtesy and indulgence (and good-natured teasing) traditionally shown newlyweds.

Q. Who will be in Jesus's army when He leads it down from Heaven?

A. Just about everyone: His forces will include not only the angels, the Old Testament saints (everyone who believed in God from Adam until the Crucifixion), and the Tribulation saints (everyone martyred for his or her belief in Jesus during the Tribulation), but *His own wife*. Yes, rather than sulk in the hotel or wander around shopping and killing time while waiting for her husband to get back, the Church will be at Jesus's side as He faces off against Satan, the Antichrist, and the False Prophet.

We think this bodes well for the success of the marriage.

CHAPTER 31

The Battles of Armageddon

The term "Battle of Armageddon" is commonly used to mean "the one final confrontation between Good and Evil." That is technically incorrect; that one, final confrontation will consist of a *series* of battles.

> According to Revelation 16:16, the Antichrist's armies will take advantage of the drying-up of the Euphrates to gather at Mount Megiddo, about six miles south of Haifa in northern Israel. Other armies will assemble there as well, as noted in a general way in Revelation 19:19. A similar mustering of evil forces is mentioned in Zechariah 14:1–2.

This is going to be the climactic event in the history of mankind—the "Glorious Appearing," the "Second Coming"—and we'd like to be there to see it. But by the end of the Seal, Trumpet, and Bowl Judgments, we think the airline industry will be even more undependable and aggravating than it is today, if such a thing is possible. That means that when the excitement gets under way, we'll be at home.

Game Time

Which doesn't mean we'll miss the "action." Even though the sun and the moon will go dark and the stars will fall out of the sky (see Matthew 24:29–31), still, the Bible tells us that "all the tribes of the earth" will "see the Son of Man coming on the clouds."

Surely this means that the Battle of Armageddon will be televised.

How else can everyone all over the globe see the same event happening at the same time? And it *should* be televised, because this showdown will be nothing less than a cross between the World Series of History and the Superbowl of Religion. The winner gets "bragging rights." For the loser, "it's all over." (And there's no "wait till next year." There is no next year.)

As with the World Series, the contest will be decided over a number of "games." And, as with the Superbowl, the Battles of Armageddon will be *the premier advertising opportunity of the year.*

Which means you should think about buying ad time on it.

As you'll see in a later chapter, we think that capitalism, commerce, money, and the private sector will disappear with the coming of the Millennium. But what if we're wrong? What if the Kingdom of Heaven on Earth consists of a consumer economy like we have now—business as usual except that Jesus is in charge? Then anyone who kept his venture going, and who put his message out during the Battle of Armageddon, will have a head start on everyone else in terms of name recognition. And that, as everyone knows, leads to brand loyalty and market share.

True, the total number of "eyeballs" you'll get from advertising on this "Superbowl Series" won't be anything like what you'd have gotten from actual MLB and NFL championships, because most of the owners of those eyeballs will be dead. But of those still alive, the numbers will be excellent—maybe 100 percent.

However, depending on your product or service, the Battles

of Armageddon may not be the right "environment" in which to present your message. To help you decide, here's a preview of what to expect.

In each game, the opposing sides consist of Jesus and the armies of Christ (the angelic hosts, the Old Testament saints, the Church, and the Tribulation saints) versus the Antichrist (indwelled by Satan), the False Prophet, the three "froglike spirits," and armies coming from the east and the west and the north and the south and composed, presumably, either of conscripted nonbelievers (including, we assume, Jews) or enthusiastic followers of the Antichrist.

THE BATTLES OF ARMAGEDDON: PRE-SERIES RUNDOWN

GAME ONE

Where: Edom (south of Judah and Moab)
Says Who: Isaiah 63:1–4 (*1: Who is this that cometh from Edom, with dyed garments from Bozrah? this that is glorious in his apparel, traveling in the greatness of his strength? I that speak in righteousness, mighty to save.*)
Play-by-Play: Unknown
Highlights: Unknown
Final Score: Jesus wins.

GAME TWO

Where: Mount (Har) Megiddo, in the Jezreel Valley
Says Who: Revelation 16:16
Play-by-Play: Revelation 19 includes an account of how an angel will invite birds to eat the bodies of the dead (*17: And I saw an angel standing in the sun; and he cried with a loud voice, saying to all the*

The Battle of Armageddon. Note hovering birds waiting to dine on flesh of kings, captains, mighty men, horses, them that sit on them, etc.

fowls that fly in the midst of heaven, Come and gather yourselves together unto the supper of the great God; 18: That ye may eat the flesh of kings, and the flesh of captains, and the flesh of mighty men, and the flesh of horses, and of them that sit on them, and the flesh of all men, both free and bond, both small and great).
Highlights: Jesus will defeat the enemy by using the sword that comes out of his mouth. See Revelation 19:21 (*And the remnant were slain with the sword of him that sat upon the horse, which sword proceeded out of his mouth: and all the fowls were filled with their flesh*).

Also, Jesus will make the flesh, tongues, and eyes of his enemies melt. Then he will set them against one another. See Zechariah 14:12–13 (*12: And this shall be the plague wherewith the LORD will smite all the people that have fought against Jerusalem; Their flesh shall consume away while they stand upon their feet, and their eyes shall consume away in their holes, and their tongue shall consume away in their mouth. 13: And it shall come to pass in that day, that a great tumult from the LORD shall be among them; and they shall lay hold every one on the hand of his neighbour, and his hand shall rise up against the hand of his neighbour).*

Controversy: How will one neighbor's hand be able to take hold of or rise up against another neighbor's hand, when both hands will have previously melted away and both neighbors will be blind?

Final Score: Jesus wins.

GAME THREE

Where: Valley of Jehoshaphat (probably the Kidron Valley, east of Jerusalem)

Says Who: Joel 3:1–2; Revelation 14:14–20

Opponent: All the nations

Play-by-Play: *"Swing the sickle, for the harvest is ripe; come, trample the grapes, for the winepress is full and the vats overflow"* (Joel 3:13). Revelation 14:14 seems to suggest that this is a "play" given Jesus by an angel as He sits on a cloud, wearing a golden crown, and refers to the massacre of the armies of the Antichrist.

Highlights: *"They were trampled in the winepress outside the city, and blood flowed out of the press, rising as high as the horses' bridles for a distance of 1,600 stadia [200 miles]"* (Revelation 14:20).

Final Score: Jesus wins.

GAME FOUR

Where: Jerusalem

Says Who: Zechariah 12:1–9; Revelation 16:17–21

Opponent: Satan/Antichrist and what is left of his armies

Play-by-Play: Jesus will make his enemies' riders insane, cause

> their horses to go blind, and "cut in pieces" everyone else who
> tries to conquer Jerusalem.
> Highlights: Tim LaHaye provides the commentary: ". . . the entire
> country will be bathed in the blood of unregenerate, God-hating,
> Christ-opposing peoples."
> Final Score: Jesus wins — a sweep!

As you can see, the series promises a lot of excitement, action,
and suspense. It also promises a lot of melting tongues, oceans
of blood, and birds eating the hacked-up bodies of humans and
horses. Think carefully before deciding it's an appropriate context for promoting your business.

FEARFULLY ASKED QUESTIONS (FAQ)

Q. I think I may want to buy ad time on the Armageddon broadcast.
How do I go about it?

A. Call up one of the networks, if there are any left. Say, "Can I buy ad
time when you show the Battles of Armageddon?" See what they say.
Then use any of the widely available video cameras and editing software to make your commercial.

Q. What will happen after all the battles?

A. Jesus will "land" on the Mount of Olives, the place from which He
originally ascended to Heaven. When His feet touch the ground, the
mountains will split in half and move in two different directions. We
know this from Zechariah 14:3–5.

Then He'll turn His attention to dealing with the Antichrist and the
False Prophet.

CHAPTER 32

Who's Sorry Now?

Although the Battle of Armageddon will be televised, we're pretty sure the judgment and punishment of the Antichrist and the False Prophet won't be. It's one thing to send a production crew to Megiddo or Jerusalem. It's another thing to send them to the Lake of Fire.

The Beast and the False Prophet Are Thrown into the Lake of Fire

The fate of the Antichrist and his chief henchman, the False Prophet, is explicitly foretold. They will be thrown, by Christ, into the Lake of Fire, as set forth in Revelation 19:20 (*And the beast was taken, and with him the false prophet that wrought miracles before him, with which he deceived them that had received the mark of the beast, and them that worshipped his image. These both were cast alive into a lake of fire burning with brimstone*).

That's gotta hurt. But suffering excruciating and agonizing torment forever and ever is the only language some people understand.

Satan Is Bound in the Abyss for 1,000 Years

Satan, obviously, has a lot to answer for and will also have to be punished. LaHaye reminds us that Satan is responsible for "the Roman Catholic Church," "the French skepticism of Voltaire and Rousseau," and "German Rationalism," as well as "evolution, psychiatry, illuminism, Nietzscheism, socialism, communism, liberalism, and Nazism."

How do you adequately punish someone like that?

> Satan will be cast into the Abyss (also known as the Bottomless Pit) and bound there, with a chain, for one thousand years, after which he will be released for a short time. All of this is foretold in Revelation 20:1–3.

In other words, Satan gets a thousand years in jail and then gets paroled. That might seem kind of outrageous—why on earth would the Devil get time off? For "good behavior"? No. As always, God has His reasons. He wants to keep Satan alive for a millennium and then give him one last "shot" at corrupting humanity.

Before we get to that, though, let's talk about mankind's reward for accepting Jesus: the Thousand-Year Reign of Christ on Earth.

Part VII Two Happy Endings

CHAPTER 33

Under New Management

With the defeat of the Antichrist, Jesus will establish His Thousand-Year Reign on Earth. First, though, we assume He'll want to rehab the property, turning the oceans and rivers back from blood into water, repairing the sun, and reinstalling the mountains that ran away, the islands that floated around, and the stars that fell from the sky.

At least, that's what we would do. God may have other plans.

The Thousand-Year Reign of Christ

The Church was resurrected during the Rapture. Now Jesus will resurrect "the Tribulation saints," those who accepted Him during the Tribulation and were killed because of it. These were the people who resisted taking the Mark® of the Antichrist, and they're the ones who will help Jesus run the world during the next thousand years. This is clearly predicted in Revelation 20:4.

As for everyone else — that is, those people throughout history who did not accept Jesus as their personal savior and who have been dead since the time of the Crucifixion — they will remain dead during the thousand-year Kingdom of Christ, as is revealed in Revelation 20:5–6.

Everyone left alive — those who accepted Christ during the

Tribulation and are still alive, and those who did not accept Him but for some reason *didn't* die — will find themselves in a world unlike any they have ever known, as is foretold in Isaiah 65:17 (*For, behold, I create new heavens and a new earth: and the former shall not be remembered, nor come into mind*).

As Tim LaHaye points out, ". . . nothing is more detrimental to humanity than religion and government . . . the Bible teaches that a government without a benevolent despot of supernatural origin as its leader cannot be a happy experience, but a source of human misery." Finally, humanity will have that benevolent supernatural despot. And, as if that weren't wonderful enough, the human race will completely forget about everything in its history leading up to that glorious day.

Meet the New Boss

If you're reading this book, you're already wondering, "What should I do to attain success during the Thousand-Year Kingdom of Christ on Earth? How can I really *get ahead* in the Millennium?"

It's a good question — and the answer may surprise you.

Before we discuss that, though, let's review what we know about what life in the Millennium will be like. For that we turn to Isaiah 65:18–25.

There will be economic stability, and everyone will enjoy the fruits of his or her own labor (*21: And they shall build houses, and inhabit them; and they shall plant vineyards, and eat the fruit of them. 22: They shall not build, and another inhabit; they shall not plant, and another eat*).

Talk about "the good old days"! Life will be like it was in the *really* good old days — the Early Paleolithic. Everyone will be self-sufficient and make his or her own food, clothing, and shelter. Because mankind will have forgotten all previous human history, there will be no capitalism, no money, no corporations, no mass production, no industrialism, no unions, no salaries or benefits or pensions . . . in fact, no *jobs.*

The result? Just what you'd expect.

> Everyone will always be happy (*19: And I will rejoice in Jerusalem, and joy in my people: and the voice of weeping shall be no more heard in her, nor the voice of crying*).

Not only will we all get to grow and eat our own grapes, but, as verse 17 says, no one will remember how life used to be, with its high cost of health insurance, and its candy bars that seemed to get smaller every time you bought one, and its appliances that always broke after a year. In fact, there probably won't be any appliances at all. If there were, we wouldn't know what to do with them and they'd have to last an unbelievably long time:

> The normal life span will be as long as it was before the Flood. Those born during the Millennium will have the first hundred years of their lives to accept Christ as Savior and Lord. Those who do so will live for a thousand years, procreating dozens, if not hundreds, of times, resulting in a world overwhelmingly populated by Christians. Those who refuse to accept Jesus will die at age one hundred. All this can be derived from Isaiah 65:20 (*There shall be no more thence an infant of days, nor an old man that hath not filled his days: for the child shall die an hundred years old; but the sinner being an hundred years old shall be accursed*).

This suggests another reason it's good that we won't remember life as it was previously lived. Our life span will be measurable in centuries (we predict that 650 will be the new 65), and that means having many, many children. The prospect of sending dozens (let alone *hundreds*) of kids to college, with tuitions and housing and textbook prices being what they are today and having a thousand years to get even higher, would turn the Millennial Kingdom into Hell on Earth. But, thank God, we won't remember what college is.

Meanwhile, it's good to know that anyone born during the Millennium who rejects Christ will die young, at age one hundred. Because to begin with, they're probably crazy. Who would reject Jesus when He's alive and living here and bringing us all this happiness? However, even though they will die, these nonbelievers will live long enough to have children and, presumably, pass their crazy nonbelief on to them. Thus, plenty of children will be born toward the end of the Kingdom, and they'll be ready, willing, and able to follow Satan when he is released from the Abyss.

Because isn't that typical? Isn't that what adolescents do? They defy their parents in immature, self-destructive ways. Like the teenagers of today, these satanic teens of the Millennium will be repulsive, vulgar, lazy, sex-crazed, drug-addled illiterates. What will we do when Lucifer leads these anti-Christian teenagers in an attack against us?

Actually, we will have one rather special ally:

God will answer prayers much more quickly than He has until now; He might even answer prayers *before* they are offered (*Isaiah 65:24: And it shall come to pass, that before they call, I will answer; and while they are yet speaking, I will hear*).

As you can see, life in the Kingdom (except for the Satan-worshipping teenagers) will be perfect, especially if you like working with wood or growing grapes. Still, there will be those ambitious individuals for whom being happy all the time, for a thousand years, just isn't enough. If you're among them, what should you do to advance your career?

Do what you'd do in a regular job: Cultivate the "boss."

We're not exactly saying "get on His good side," since the boss, in this case, is, of course, the Son of God, Jesus Christ. His good side is His *only* side—even after bloody battling. Rather, we're saying: Make yourself indispensable. Go the extra mile to make sure His needs are fulfilled. It will pay off, believe us. Even a benevolent supernatural despot needs a staff.

How can you advance your own career by serving Him and helping to advance His? We have some basic tips:

1. **Move to where He lives.** We have no idea, but it might be Jerusalem. Or maybe Nazareth—He's "from" there, so He might want to establish His official headquarters in His hometown to "give something back" to the community. In any case, once the Millennium gets under way, everyone will know where He is.

2. Discreetly and unobtrusively, see if you can **find out His schedule**—what restaurants He goes to for lunch (and maybe breakfast), whether He gets a newspaper at the same spot every morning, and so on. Jesus may, for instance, have a predictable health club routine.

3. Taking care not to neglect your house-building and grape-growing responsibilities, try to be in places where you can **"accidentally" run into Him.** Don't be shy about introducing yourself. He already knows who you are, and He knows that you know who He is.

4. **Make yourself useful.** Sure, He'll already have a lot of assistants and interns. But who knows how good they'll be?

Remember, He may be Jesus Christ, but He'll be running what is in essence the biggest start-up in history. In the beginning, for the first two or three hundred years, He'll need all the help He can get.

"Accidentally" running into Jesus. Offering hard copy of résumé is a nice touch—
with the entire world to run, even Jesus is going to need help.

Satan Is Released One Last Time

A thousand years after Christ begins His millennial reign, Satan
will be released from the Abyss for a final round of evildoing, as
is revealed in Revelation 20:7 (*And when the thousand years are
expired, Satan shall be loosed out of his prison*).

You might wonder: Why would anyone release him? He's *Satan*,
for God's sake. We know how he operates. As soon as he gets
out, he'll go back to "deceiving the nations," which means everything from fomenting rebellion against God to encouraging
man to double-park. Why will God give him the chance?

As we mentioned, the reason is so that the final generation of
mankind, born less than one hundred years before the end of the
Millennium, will have its own opportunity to choose between the
Devil and Jesus. Of course, given that choice, we know which *we*
think is the obviously better option. But we'll have been Christians for a thousand years and about three months, so we can
hardly claim to be objective.

Scripture, in Revelation 20:8, says that many will follow Satan. He *"shall go out to deceive the nations which are in the four quarters of the earth, Gog and Magog, to gather them together to battle: the number of whom is as the sand of the sea."*

This final battle will be brief. Gog and Magog will surround the believing Christians, but then fire will come from Heaven and destroy them. All this is clearly predicted in Revelation 20:9 (*And they went up on the breadth of the earth, and compassed the camp of the saints about, and the beloved city: and fire came down from God out of heaven, and devoured them*).

There is complete confusion over what "Gog and Magog" refers to, but here we think they are probably general terms for "those who worship false gods." The names have also been used by theologians and religious commentators to denote places and specific persons.

In any case, it's hard to see how Gog and Magog could "encompass the camp of the saints," since the human race will have just spent the past thousand years populating the world with almost nothing but Fundamentalist Christians, while the nonbelievers will have been automatically dying when they reach one hundred. Maybe Gog and Magog are the names of two specific individuals who worship false gods. Two guys with funny names, arrayed against billions of the faithful and Jesus Himself: How dangerous can they be?

In any case, it all turns out okay in the end.

CHAPTER 34

You're Fired

Satan Thrown into the Lake of Fire Forever

> After his final defeat, Satan will be cast into the Lake of Fire, to
> join the Antichrist and the False Prophet for an eternity of tor-
> ment. This is foretold in Revelation 20:10 (*And the devil that
> deceived them was cast into the lake of fire and brimstone, where
> the beast and the false prophet are, and shall be tormented day
> and night for ever and ever*).

Finally.

Okay, then. Enough already with Satan. He's done.

The next chapter is the final chapter—of this book, of
mankind's history, of the story of humanity's relationship with
God. Like so many of the seminal events in our history, it all
comes down to real estate: The eternal dwelling place of both
mankind and God will be a cross between a walled city and a
gigantic condo.

But first, there is the important matter of punishing those who
rejected Jesus.

The Great White Throne Judgment

We come now to the final judgment of mankind. It is so monu-
mentally important that even John, the author of the book of

Revelation, seems to have been intimidated by his vision of it and lost his bearings, because it ends on a highly confusing note.

> At this final Judgment, God will be seated on a big white throne, as set forth in Revelation 20:11 (*And I saw a great white throne, and him that sat on it, from whose face the earth and the heaven fled away; and there was found no place for them*).

People may wonder: Why does God need to sit down? Answer: Because He's tired, just as He was on the seventh day after creating the universe, when He had to rest. In fact, God is the only one in Heaven who is *allowed* to sit down.

> Before Him will be the souls of the dead. The dead will come from the sea, from Hell, and from death, to be judged by what they did during their lifetime. This is set forth in Revelation 20:12–13 (*12: And I saw the dead, small and great, stand before God; and the books were opened: and another book was opened, which is the book of life: and the dead were judged out of those things which were written in the books, according to their works. 13: And the sea gave up the dead which were in it; and death and hell delivered up the dead which were in them: and they were judged every man according to their works*).

God will have in front of Him a set of books. These billions of volumes record everything every individual did during his or her lifetime. This is perhaps what high school guidance counselors—who traditionally take the long view—refer to when they talk about your "permanent record."

It seems as though God reads from "the books," which record everyone's deeds, and then, based on those deeds, does or doesn't inscribe an individual's name in the Book of Life.

Everyone whose name is not "written in the book of life" will be cast into the Lake of Fire and will stay there forever and ever, as set forth in Revelation 20:14–15 (*14: And death and hell were cast into the lake of fire. This is the second death. 15: And whosoever was not found written in the book of life was cast into the lake of fire*).

It seems fair enough: God judges you on what you did in your life and rewards or punishes you accordingly. But our End Times experts say that one's deeds in life *don't* determine whether you get eternal life or unending torment. What matters is whether you have accepted Jesus—i.e., salvation by faith, not by works.

Thus, they say that this "book of life" is really *two* books. One is the Book of Life, which is merely the book containing the names of those who, at any given moment, are alive. The other is the Lamb's Book of Life (which is mentioned in Revelation 21:27), which is more important. It contains only the names of those who "call on the Lamb for salvation," i.e., who have accepted Christ.

This is fine with us because, as you know, by now we'll have called on the Lamb for salvation big-time. The only thing we wonder is, if it's true that God ignores your "works," why does Revelation mention "works" not once but twice?

But never mind. Such a matter is, as they say, "above our pay grade." The good news in all this is that after Satan's final defeat, Death itself, and Hell itself, will be destroyed. Death will go to Hell and Hell will drop dead. So to speak.

CHAPTER 35

The New Heaven and Earth

The Millennium has ended. It's time for humanity, or at least part of it, to live happily ever after.

Once evil and sin are forever vanquished, God will create a brand-new Heaven and Earth for the enjoyment of mankind. He will begin by destroying the old Heaven and Earth, as foretold in Revelation 21:1 (*And I saw a new heaven and a new earth: for the first heaven and the first earth were passed away; and there was no more sea*).

It's too bad the real estate market won't exist anymore, because—talk about "location, location, location"—one very special neighborhood is going to be welcoming one very special celebrity neighbor. Jesus has lived on Earth for a thousand years, but now God Himself is moving in.

God will move out of Heaven and actually live on Earth with man, forever, as revealed in Revelation 21:3 (*And I heard a great voice out of heaven saying, Behold, the tabernacle of God is with men, and he will dwell with them, and they shall be his people, and God himself shall be with them, and be their God*).

We wonder: Will Jesus stay on Earth, too? He would have to, right? Where else can He live, now that God is closing down Heaven?

> After creating the planet anew, God will create a city for everyone to live in. It will come down out of the sky, fully ready for habitation, as noted in Revelation 21:2 (*And I John saw the holy city, new Jerusalem, coming down from God out of heaven, prepared as a bride adorned for her husband*).

Interestingly, there may still be nonbelievers left alive. Say you were born in the year 901 of the Millennium. Technically you would have until age one hundred to accept or reject Jesus, which would take you to the year 1001, by which time the New Jerusalem will have arrived. We think that any nonbeliever born after 900 will "get a free pass" to exist on Earth—but not, of course, to dwell among Christians (or to be near God). Instead, we think they will comprise other nations.

> Assuming all living Christians will abide in the New Jerusalem, we subscribe to the New International Version of the Bible, which says, in Revelation 21:24, *The nations will walk by its light, and the kings of the earth will bring their splendor into it.* In 21:27 it adds, *Nothing impure will ever enter it, nor will anyone who does what is shameful or deceitful, but only those whose names are written in the Lamb's book of Life.*

Of course we find it disturbing to know that there might be whole nations of young whippersnappers less than a hundred years old, worshipping other gods and doing Christ-knows-what (and obedient to their "kings") elsewhere. We will believe, and will have no difficulty in proclaiming, that Earth is a *Christian planet*. But these other nations may actually turn out to be a blessing. Christians who like to travel will at least have an array of potential destinations where they can broaden their horizons and expose themselves to other cultures, before hurrying back home to paradise.

The Last Condo

The New Jerusalem will be immense, providing ample space for the estimated 20 billion people who will occupy it.

> The city will have the dimensions of a cube, of equal length along its three dimensions. Each side will be 12,000 stadia, as set forth in Revelation 21:15–16 (*And he that talked with me had a golden reed to measure the city, and the gates thereof, and the wall thereof. 16: And the city lieth foursquare, and the length is as large as the breadth: and he measured the city with the reed, twelve thousand furlongs [stadia]. The length and the breadth and the height of it are equal*).

The New Jerusalem. Drawn almost to scale. Placement over continental United States is for illustrative purposes only, as we do not know where it will set down after its descent from Heaven (not shown).

Some translations employ the archaic *stadia,* and some say *furlongs.* They're synonymous. In standard definitions, one furlong equals 660 feet, or one-eighth of a mile. Thus, 12,000 furlongs equals about 1,500 miles. (Our New International Version of the Bible says it's the equivalent of about 1,400 miles.) We are discussing, therefore, a building that will be 1,400 to 1,500 miles long, wide, and high. This will be, to put it mildly, a hell of a big structure.

Every person will get his or her own residential unit. LaHaye notes, "My friend and colleague Dr. Henry M. Morris, an expert engineer and author, has done the math on this and concluded that given the estimated population of possibly twenty billion residents, each person would enjoy a block of space of approximately one cubic mile, or its length, breadth, and height would be 'a little over a third of a mile in each direction.' " Isn't that typical? The ground hasn't even been broken for this project, and already the hype is starting. In fact, a cube measuring one-third of a mile in each direction would only encompass one-twenty-seventh of a cubic mile. Either someone in Sales is exaggerating the size of our prospective units, or Dr. Henry M. Morris is an engineer in the sense that he can drive a train. In any case, a cubic mile would, by definition, be one mile each in length, breadth, and height.

We've done the correct math on this, and here it is: Figuring 1,400 miles on each side, a cube housing 20 billion people in individual units would allot a space of .137 cubic miles per person, which is to say, a cubic space a little over half a mile in each direction. True, it's not a mile in each direction. But after the first hundred acres, how much more floor space do you need? (Each unit's total area would be about 160 acres.)

Even if everyone's apartment ends up being slightly smaller than that, to allow for corridors, HVAC installation, elevators, utility spaces, common rooms (for catered lunches, "affairs," amateur talent show nights, et cetera), and a huge, splendid front lobby with ballrooms and meeting rooms on the ground floor, still—go complain. It would take a thousand years just to put together enough Ikea bookshelves to line the walls of one unit. It's a nice setup.

And ambitious, too. But then, we expect nothing less from its designer. Who but God could conceive of and build a city that extends six hundred miles past the outermost layer of Earth's atmosphere? And look at these unique specs:

> The city will be made of precious stones and metals, as foretold in Revelation 21:19 and 21:21 (*19: And the foundations of the wall of the city were garnished with all manner of precious stones. . . . 21: And the twelve gates were twelve pearls; every several gate was of one pearl: and the street of the city was pure gold, as it were transparent glass*).

It sounds lovely, and we can't wait to move in. But we were a little confused at first over whether to think of this place as a city or building. Finally, since we'll be actually living in it, we decided to think of it as a building.

We suggest you do the same—which means exercising a little due diligence. When it comes time to move into the New Jerusalem, make sure you ask the same kinds of questions you would when shopping for a condominium. ("The New Jerusalem" even sounds like a condo complex.) In this way, you can be sure to get the most for your money and maximize your unit's resale value.

Of course, by the time it's ready for habitation, there may be no such thing as "money," "resale," or "value." But you never know. So here are a few tips. Clip and save.

The New Jerusalem: Questions to Ask Before Move-In

1. Ask to see a copy of the CC&R's (Covenants, Conditions, and Restrictions) to know what is and what is not allowed regarding noise, smells, smoking, and the requirements of hygiene for individual units. (Remember that God is the owner, developer, and manager. When He says "covenant" He means it.) Be sure the document is in a language you speak, and don't be afraid to ask for clarifications of passages that employ excessive "legalese" or Aramaic.

2. Are pets allowed? If so, what kinds? Can you breed livestock — or, more important, can your neighbors? Is there any size limit to flocks or herds?

3. What changes can you make to the property? Can you subdivide it into new rooms or erect new buildings? Can you build a loft bed? Can you add a water bed? Can you grow little pots of fresh herbs or, on a larger scale, cultivate wheat or corn?

4. Can you conduct any other kind of hobby or quasi-business activities on the property, including light manufacturing, brewing and/or distilling, artistic activities (painting, sculpture, et cetera), and music or dramatic rehearsals or productions?

5. Be clear what everyone's rights and responsibilities are with regard to the common areas. For example, if — as is possible, given occupancy of 20 billion — more than one resident wants to use the auxiliary room for a birthday party, how is it decided which resident gets it?

6. Inquire about expanding into other units. This is highly unlikely, of course, since probably no one will move out, and no one will die. But it's good to know if you can acquire an adjacent space and "break through," just in case.

7. Will swapping units be permitted? If, say, after five million years, you and occupant X are tired of your respective locations and wish to trade, will you be allowed?

8. Who will manage the structure? Will they be appointed, elected, anointed, or what? Will their jurisdiction be defined by floor? By wing? Or will God (Who can do anything) manage the whole thing?

9. Does every resident have to live alone, rattling around in a living room a quarter of a square mile? What if you want to live with someone? Can you combine units?

10. With these nondying tenants having babies, what happens when, after a few generations, it's so crowded that no one can breathe, despite its being perfect?

11. How will specific floors be assigned or awarded? Is there any way to assure either a higher or lower floor?

This last point is especially important if, say, you like to take walks.

The benefits of an upper-floor location, for example, might include spectacular views of the planet Earth, an unimpeded vista of the cosmos, and the ability to lean out a window and spit watermelon seeds on the Hubble telescope as it orbits at its puny altitude of a mere 350 miles above sea level. But even the most devoted stargazer might occasionally want to enjoy some recreational activities out in nature. That will mean leaving the building and exiting through the gates of the city to gain access to the surrounding countryside.

However, getting out of the building may be something of an ordeal. Unless God will allow us to teleport ourselves instantly over long distances, or to grow wings and fly like the angels, we'll have to get up and down the New Jerusalem in a mechanical conveyance. If each person gets a space half a mile in each dimension, then each floor is half a mile high. That means the New Jerusalem will feature between 2,800 and 3,000 floors. Hence, traveling from, say, the 2,418th floor to ground level will be roughly the equivalent of riding an elevator from Baltimore to Dallas. Moving at the highest downward speed available to elevators today, such a trip would take 2.6 days.

But that's nonstop. And, of course, there would be stops.

Slowing, halting, and resuming eight or nine hundred times on the way down doesn't sound like fun, especially as the elevator gets increasingly crowded and everybody feels that slight tension and awkwardness you feel in elevators. So bring a book to read, and perhaps a tent and a sleeping bag. And hope you get a lower floor.

The Last Cruise

Then again, most people might simply choose never to leave. Like on a cruise, everything anyone will need will be right there, provided for free.

> This metropolis will need no celestial or artificial sources of illumination because God will be the source of light. For this reason, there will be no need for a sun or a moon. But then, it's just as well that there will be no moon, because there will never again be night. All this is clearly predicted in Revelation 21:23 and 21:25 (*23: And the city had no need of the sun, neither of the moon, to shine in it: for the glory of God did lighten it, and the Lamb is the light thereof. . . . 25: And the gates of it shall not be shut at all by day: for there shall be no night there*).
>
> Humans will still need water, so an endless supply of it will issue from the throne of God Himself, as revealed in Revelation

22:1 (*And he shewed me a pure river of water of life, clear as crystal, proceeding out of the throne of God and of the Lamb*). For food, various trees will provide different fruits every month, as promised in Revelation 22:2 (*In the midst of the street of it, and on either side of the river, was there the tree of life, which bare twelve manner of fruits, and yielded her fruit every month: and the leaves of the tree were for the healing of the nations*).

(It says "a pure river of water of life." *Aquavit* also means "water of life" and is a kind of vodka distilled from potatoes or grain and flavored with herbs, especially caraway seeds. Maybe that's what will issue from God's throne or drip out of Jesus! Although it's probably just regular, albeit perfect, water.)

If "the leaves of the tree" will be "for the healing of the nations," then that, too, suggests that other groups of nonbelievers will populate the Earth, since those of us living in the New Jerusalem won't need leaves or healing because we'll never get sick. In fact, some wonder whether we'll even have what we are used to calling "bodies."

We certainly hope we'll have bodies, because we know we're going to have heads.

Everyone will wear the seal of God on his or her forehead. Indeed, God Himself will have a head, or at least a face, since people will be able to see it, as revealed in Revelation 22:4 (*And they shall see his face; and his name shall be in their foreheads*).

It might seem too good to be true, that you can be out visiting a friend one day and actually see God—His face and everything—in what would of course amount to the most stupendous celebrity sighting imaginable. But it's not only possible, and even probable, it's more or less inevitable. Remember that with the opening of the New Jerusalem, time (or, rather, Time) itself will come to a halt. Life in this ultimate high-rise, with Jesus and God and all the saints, will go on for eternity.

Sooner or later you've got to bump into Him.

The End?

We've come, at last, to our final "return on investment."

All of human history, and in fact all of the history of the entire universe, has been leading up to this. No matter how you lived and what you did (or didn't do), as long as you accepted Jesus, you will become a part of "the eternal order."

Up until now we've used that term to refer to our experience waiting for chicken marsala at a certain restaurant in Sherman Oaks. But soon it will mean something completely different. It will refer to the state of paradise for which generations of the faithful have been yearning and praying—and, sometimes, dying—for thousands of years. This is mankind's glorious and triumphant apotheosis, and we can't wait to be a part of it.

Of course, the physical aspects of the New Jerusalem, as described above, speak for themselves and have prompted us to redefine our idea of "heaven on Earth." But life in any real Heaven has to include more than just a nice residence. God, of course, knows this. And that's why He's made sure that the New Heaven will be everything it should be, and more.

Just imagine:

We will be eternally happy in a city populated exclusively by people exactly like us. There will be no Catholics, or Muslims, or Jews. There will be no Hindus, Taoists, Buddhists, Eastern Orthodox Christians, Christian Scientists, Mormons, animists, pantheists, polytheists, Baha'is, Confucians, Jains, or Shintoists.

We think, although sometimes we get confused, that there will be no, or almost no, Calvinists, Methodists, Lutherans, Jehovah's

Witnesses, Presbyterians, Episcopalians, Anabaptists, Quakers, Unitarians, Seventh-Day Adventists, or Moravians.

Oh, and it almost goes without saying that there will be no homosexuals.

And it's not just their absence (plus the absence of all atheists, Amish, Mennonites, Sikhs, agnostics, Scientologists, "Moonies," Wiccans, witches, warlocks, New Age-ists, Eckists, Native Americans, Deists, Spiritualists, and pretty much everyone else who ever lived, including many Baptists) that will be so gratifying and delightful. We will also derive a sense of vindication, satisfaction, and righteous affirmation from the knowledge that all of them (no matter what they did during their lives) have been judged to be as evil as Satan himself, since they will have been punished as he was, condemned to suffer indescribable agony for all time in the Lake of Fire.

We, meanwhile, will be living not just "the good life" but the *great* life. It's all been laid out for us by a prophet from a tribal desert society writing in exile on a tiny Greek island two thousand years ago, before anyone had ever heard of checkbooks, wholesale, initial public offerings, or the Pacific Ocean.

And you can be there with us. Don't despair if the Rapture comes and you're left behind. If you follow the advice in these pages, there's a good chance you'll be able to survive and even flourish during the worst period in human history. And remember that as the prophecies come true one by one, you can decide for yourself when you're convinced that the author of Revelation knew what he was talking about. Then just do what we will have done: Abandon your previous beliefs, accept Jesus as your personal savior, and stay inside, away from invisible locusts and moving mountains.

In time you'll get to the Millennium and a thousand years of smooth sailing. And after that? We'll see you on move-in day as we share a Christian mystic's vision of paradise: dwelling hundreds of miles above the Earth along with Tim LaHaye (and his wife, Beverly), Dr. Henry M. Morris, Pat Robertson, Jerry Falwell, Tom DeLay, Bill Frist, Pastor John Hagee, Mitch McConnell, Rick Santorum, John Kyl, Dennis Hastert, Roy Blunt, John Ashcroft, Ralph Reed, James Dobson, Paul Weyrich, Glenn Beck, Jack (and Rexella) Van Impe, Mike Huckabee, and 20 billion like them, in perpetual daylight, praising God, drinking water, and eating fruit.

Forever.

Our Sources

Our sources include various Web sites and the following publications:

Bussard, Dave. *Who Will Be Left Behind and When?* (2002, Strong Tower Publishing)

Currie, David B. *Rapture: The End-Times Error That Leaves the Bible Behind* (2003, Sophia Institute Press)

Hitchcock, Mark, and Thomas Ice. *The Truth Behind Left Behind: A Biblical View of the End Times* (2004, Multnomah Publishers)

LaHaye, Tim. *Revelation Unveiled* (1999, Zondervan) This is a revised and updated edition of *Revelation Illustrated and Made Plain*, 1973.

Lindsey, Hal. *The Late Great Planet Earth* (1970, Zondervan)

Rosenthal, Marvin. *The Pre-Wrath Rapture of the Church* (1990, Thomas Nelson Publishers)

Sutton, Hilton. *Rapture: Get Right or Get Left* (1991, Harrison House)

Of these authors, the two best-known are Hal Lindsey and Tim LaHaye. Lindsey's book was the first contemporary exploration of End Times phenomena to reach a wide audience; his book has sold more than 35 million copies even though none of its warnings or predictions has come true in almost four decades. LaHaye is a minister active in conservative politics and coauthor of the hugely popular Left Behind series. His book about Revelation was first published in 1973. The version we used is a "revised and updated" version published in 1999, although how you update a commentary on a two-thousand-year-old text is something of a mystery.

We were frustrated to discover that the more we researched the specifics of the Rapture and the Tribulation in these books and Web sites and in the Bible itself, the less unanimity we found. In fact, no two sources agreed on very much of anything—chronology, duration, who invades whom, who descends from Heaven and preaches where, et cetera. So we stopped trying to reconcile them and chose the account set forth in LaHaye's *Revelation Unveiled*. We would ask only that readers more knowledgeable about these matters, or who have a different view of the specifics, forgive us, as it were, our trespasses.

Biblical quotations are taken either from here: http://etext.lib .virginia.edu/kjv.browse.html or from *The Holy Bible, New International Version* (1984, Zondervan Bible Publishers).

Acknowledgments

Many thanks to Terry Adams, for sharing the inspiration; Paul Bresnick, for shepherding the deal; Junie Dahn, for seizing the torch; John Parsley, for leading us into the promised land; Betsy Uhrig, for cleansing the manuscript of sins; and Katherine Yurica, for counsel and guidance. We have profited greatly from all their good works.

About the Authors

Steve and Evie Levy are the fictional creations of Ellis Weiner and Barbara Davilman. Coauthors of the bestselling *Yiddish with Dick and Jane, Yiddish with George and Laura, How to Raise a Jewish Dog*, and the forthcoming *Arffirmations: Meditations for Dogs*, Ellis Weiner is also author of *Drop Dead, My Lovely; The Big Boat to Bye-Bye;* and *Santa Lives: Five Conclusive Arguments for the Existence of Santa Claus;* and Barbara Davilman is a writer for television and movies and a coeditor of the forthcoming anthology *What Was I Thinking?* She and Ellis live in Los Angeles. And yes, they are married.

About the Artist

Mark Adam Abramowicz has worked in television as an art director, casting director, writer, and director. He currently works in global marketing and advertising. This is his "illustratorial" debut.